A
Harlequin
Romance

OTHER
Harlequin Romances

by FLORA KIDD

Many of these titles are available at your local bookseller,
or through the Harlequin Reader Service.

For a free catalogue listing all available Harlequin Romances,
send your name and address to:

HARLEQUIN READER SERVICE,
M.P.O. Box 707, Niagara Falls, N.Y. 14302
Canadian address: Stratford, Ontario, Canada N5A 6W4

THE SUMMER WIFE

by

FLORA KIDD

Harlequin Books

TORONTO • LONDON • NEW YORK • AMSTERDAM • SYDNEY • WINNIPEG

Original hardcover edition published in 1976
by Mills & Boon Limited

ISBN 0-373-01999-8

Harlequin edition published August, 1976

Printed in Canada

CHAPTER ONE

On a sunny Saturday morning in early June Deirdre Lane walked down Regent Street in London, letting sunshine, blue skies, and a day off have their usual heart-lifting effect on her. Today something different would happen; something which would change the whole of her life, something strange and romantic.

Deirdre smiled to herself, a small self-mocking smile, as she recognised the hopeful feeling. Wasn't it time she grew out of such things? They belonged to childhood and adolescence and she was an adult in years at least, even if her heart was still youthful and could still leap with joy.

Colour and design in the decoration of a shop window caught her eye and she stopped to stare. The theme of the window-dressing was summer holidays, and through the shining pane of plate glass she could see faceless, rigid models in various kinds of clothes. Suits for travelling; gaily coloured swimsuits and bikinis; pretty flowered dresses and shady sunhats; elegant evening gowns.

The models were arranged against a background of blown-up photographs of Greece. There were the Parthenon and Delphi, both of which Deirdre had visited the previous summer. The tall sail of a yacht leaned forward before a strong breeze off the harbour at Rhodes, which she had also visited.

She passed on to the next window and pressed her nose against the pane so as to see better. Salzburg and the Mozart statue; Vienna, its Opera House and the wonderful woods. She had also been to Austria, last holiday but one. In fact it seemed to her that there were very few of the better-known tourist attractions on the continent of Europe that she had not visited during the past few years as she took advantage of school trips and student tours.

This year she would be going on holiday with Elise Downie, her flat-mate and colleague, but they had not yet decided where to go.

With plenty of time to stand and stare she dawdled on to the next window, which framed scenes of Scotland, the models suitably dressed for a temperate climate in glowing tweeds and fine woollens. In particular a long dress made from green wool, with a scooped neckline edged with colourful embroidery, caught her attention. How lovely to wear a dress like that and to dine by candlelight in a castle dining hall with a handsome man! Again Deirdre's small self-mocking smile which, although she did not realise it, always made her seem mysterious and tantalising, curved her mouth; she didn't know any handsome men.

But the blown-up pictures of Holyrood Palace in Edinburgh, of Balmoral Castle, of a brawny-armed man in a kilt tossing a caber at the Highland Games, kept her at the window. Perhaps she and Elise should do a tour of Scotland? After all, she had always been fascinated by the turbulent history of its people, and the scenery of mountains, glens, castles and remote sea-washed islands held a romantic allure.

She was admiring a swathe of glowing tartan when she noticed in the window the reflection of a woman passing by along the street; a tall woman whose smooth blonde hair shimmered in the sunlight and who was wearing a close-fitting tobacco-coloured suit. Recognising her, Deirdre turned and began to hurry after the quickly walking figure.

'Toni,' she called, 'wait for me!'

The woman turned to look back, and then waited.

'Dee!' she exclaimed. 'How are you? I haven't seen you for ages.'

'Last September, at your flat. You had a party. I'd just come up to town,' said Deirdre, her eyes shining with pleasure at this meeting with an old friend. 'I've phoned you several times, but you've always been away. Can you talk for a while? Perhaps we could have coffee over there at that café. I've heaps to tell you.'

This wasn't exactly true, but Deirdre was determined to keep Toni with her long enough to exchange confidences as they had always done when schoolgirls.

Toni's amber-coloured, dark-fringed eyes widened, as if she doubted that anything Deidre had to say could possibly hold her interest. Then she looked at her watch.

'All right,' she murmured, 'I've half an hour to spare before I rush off to Heathrow. I'm on the Transatlantic run.'

'Then you're still an air stewardess?' queried Deirdre as they crossed the street.

'Still, but I'm hoping to change all that fairly soon; in a few weeks, probably.' Toni gave the impression that the alternative she had in mind was far more exciting than what she was doing now. 'What about you? Teaching a lot of dumb teenagers at that girls' school, I suppose?'

'Yes, but they're not dumb. Mostly they're very bright and I have a hard time keeping ahead of them. I've had a very interesting year so far. I really enjoy my job.'

Toni's finely-plucked eyebrows made arches of surprise as she pushed open the door of the café.

'Good for you,' she observed. Then her mischievous grin turned up the corners of her mouth and for a moment Deirdre felt she was fifteen again, and back in the schoolroom. 'Do you remember the awful time we used to give old Tommy in the history lessons, when we were in the fifth form at Brunton Vale?' added Toni.

'You did, I didn't,' retorted Deirdre with a grin, as she slid into a seat at a table set for two. 'I always felt sorry for her.'

'Deirdre, the compassionate,' mocked Toni. 'Always on the side of the underdog or the maltreated. Still, I seem to remember I found that compassion of yours quite useful at times. You could always be counted on to help me out when I was in a jam—you even did my homework for me when I had something more exciting to do. I was grateful. Did I

7

ever say so?'

'If you didn't you paid back by thinking up something interesting to do, and invited me along to do it with you, and that always made up for any lack of thanks,' Deirdre replied sincerely, and again Toni's eyebrows arched in surprise. 'You've always had a magic ability to make life seem exciting.'

'Well, thanks, love,' said Toni with a little chuckle. 'For that I'll treat you to this coffee.'

They gave their orders to a waitress. The smell of coffee beans being ground and the buzz of conversation from other coffee drinkers created an atmosphere of cheerful sociability which heightened Deirdre's hopeful mood. Unbuttoning her suit jacket, she leaned back in her chair and waited for the magic to work.

'You don't change much, Dee,' Toni said as she selected a cigarette from a glit case and lit it. 'Sorry, love. Do you?' She belatedly offered the case to Deirdre, who declined. 'You still don't know what clothes to wear.'

'Oh,' Deirdre glanced down at the beige-coloured blouse she was wearing with her dark brown suit, 'I thought I looked all right. I've never pretended to be elegant like you.'

'But you could be—you're tall, you have presence. It's your hair. What are you doing with it all bunched up like that at the back of your neck?'

'It's very long,' said Deirdre almost apologetically, 'I have to put it somewhere.'

'But not in a bun! It's so ageing with your shape of face. You should have one of those new cuts, curving to the shape of the head, all sleek and shining; pluck your eyebrows which are too thick and heavy, wear a close-fitting green shirt to show off your beautiful bosom and to match your eyes, and you'd slay 'em.'

'Slay whom?' asked Deirdre coolly, stirring sugar into her coffee.

'The men, love, the men,' responded Toni, and once again her grin appeared as she watched an expression of

8

distaste flit across Deirdre's open, expressive face.

'But I don't want to slay any men,' replied Deirdre stiffly, looking down her nose. 'Why do you refer to men as if they were enemies in a battle who have to be tricked and then caught? I see them as human beings who can suffer just as we do, and whose feelings can be just as easily hurt.'

Toni stared at her for a moment and then burst out laughing so that her fine teeth glinted and her amber eyes danced with merriment. Several people in the café turned to look at her; the glances of the men lingered, Deirdre noticed.

'Oh, Dee, how prim you are!' Toni was still chuckling. 'Are you never going to have any fun out of life?'

'If I have to dress up and turn myself into a sex object to have fun, then the answer is no, I'm not going to have any fun. I refuse to go out of my way to attract men like that. It isn't playing fair. Anyway, I'd like to be appreciated for other qualities, not just the way I look.'

Toni's eyes narrowed thoughtfully as she looked through a haze of cigarette smoke.

'You know, I've always been surprised that you turned out to be a brain and won a scholarship,' she said. 'When you were a kid you used to love playing with dolls and making believe you had a house, and then you were a staunch upholder of marriage in those arguments we used to have with the other girls at school. You really believed it could work.'

'It worked for my parents, so why shouldn't I believe in it,' countered Deirdre. 'And it's still preferable to any other arrangement, if you can find someone you'd like to live with for the rest of your life.'

'And my guess is that you haven't yet. Wasn't there anyone amongst all those students at university?'

'No, not one. As a matter of fact I was too busy studying to socialise much,' replied Deirdre, thinking back to her student days when her one ambition had been to achieve high marks in order to please her parants and justify their faith in her scholastic abilities. She had achieved those marks, but by the time she had graduated her parents had not been alive to show their pleasure. And now there were times when her spirits were low, and she wondered if she had been too diligent in her studies and in the process had denied herself much of the fun which she should have enjoyed.

'Do you go out much now?' Toni asked. 'It must be awfully dull working with girls and women all day. Wouldn't you prefer to teach in a mixed school?'

'I've never really thought about it,' admitted Deirdre. 'And I don't find it dull—some of the members of staff are very clever and interesting. What about you, Toni? You said before that you might change your job soon. What are you going to do?' Deirdre spoke urgently. Time was slipping by and nothing exciting had happened yet.

Toni's smile was tantalisingly secretive.

'I'm making plans,' she replied evasively. 'Look. I must go now. Why don't you come in the taxi with me? I could drop you off at your place, it's on the way. Are you doing anything this afternoon?'

'No, not really,' mumbled Deirdre hopefully.

'Then perhaps you could do something for me?' said Toni.

Tempted by the possibility that anything Toni might ask her to do would probably be far more interesting than anything she could think up for herself, Deirdre followed her friend out of the café. Toni's effervescent personality, her elegant good looks and her overwhelming self-confidence, had always unlocked doors into worlds which she could never have entered on her own.

Soon they were in the dark tobacco-scented back seat of a taxi as it drove past Marble Arch and headed west, dodging in and out of the Saturday traffic.

'A friend of mine is in hospital here, in London. He's a photographer used to do fashion stuff, but is now freelance and does what he likes. He went with that climbing expedition to the Himalayas to photograph the mountains.'

Toni was talking quickly. Her face was a smooth un-

10

emotional mask and her golden eyes flickered as they looked out of the window at the passing scene.

'Not the expedition where some of the climbers fell and were frozen to death?' gasped Deirdre, who had read a report of the accident in a newspaper.

'One died. The other survived ... just,' Toni nodded. 'He's still recovering from severe exposure. I promised to visit him regularly, but the flight schedules have made it difficult, and he'd be glad to have another visitor—preferably female. You see, he hasn't any family. Would you go and visit him for me, Dee. please? This weekend and next week?'

'What's his name?'

'Rory Mallon. He was probably at that party of mine. Tall and tough, wild as a hawk, unconventional, always doing the unexpected.' Toni's mouth curved in a reminiscent smile as if she had good memories of her injured friend.

Deirdre was remembering a lean angular face, a mouth carved in ruthless lines, with long narrow eyes under slanting derisive eyebrows, rough rust-brown hair and a husky voice which had made fun of her. She had not liked him or his behaviour at all.

'I remember,' she said coldly, 'I thought you and he were. . . .'

'We had an arrangement,' cut in Toni swiftly, 'we'd get together when we were both in town. He's the sort who doesn't like being tied down. I met him at another party at the house of Louise Bolton, who's the sister of one of the other stewardesses. You may remember Louise—she was all the rage as a fashion model a few years ago. You could say Rory made her name and she made his.'

Deirdre was silent. She thought of the photographs which had made Louise Bolton's fair beauty famous and she cringed inwardly from going to visit the man who had taken them.

'There. That's the name of the hospital and the number of the ward.' Toni was pushing a piece of paper into her hands. 'It'll help me no end, Dee, if you'll go and visit him.'

Once again Toni was thrusting aside a responsibility she was finding irksome, thusting it on to her. But she didn't have to take it.

'I'll try, but I'm not promising,' she replied as the taxi slowed down.

'You'll go,' said Toni confidently, 'you were always a softie when it came to helping anyone who had been hurt. If you don't go. . . .' She broke off. Deirdre looked at her anxiously.

'Yes, go on,' she urged, 'what will happen if I don't go?'

'I hate to think what Rory might do,' murmured Toni in a low voice, and Deirdre felt the familiar slow stir of compassion. 'Here's your place, Dee,' Toni reminded her. 'It's been nice seeing you! I'll give you a ring some time when I'm off duty. Goodbye.'

'Goodbye, Toni.'

Elise was away for the week-end and the flat had an empty deserted atmosphere. Deirdre made herself some sandwiches and coffee and sat by the window in the sunlight to eat. Weekends had always been difficult for her to fill since she had started work last Steptember, because she had no parents to visit and her few friends usually had commitments of their own. It was true she could have gone to Berkshire to stay with Aunt Irene and Uncle Bert, but she had gone there last weekend and they wouldn't be expecting her again until next weekend.

She tried to read a book she had picked up at the library, but her mind would keep wandering to Toni's request that she should vist Rory Mallon. An image of him the last time she had seen him came into her mind; tall vigorous, possessing a rough compelling glamour. Not that she had been attracted. Quite the reverse, in fact—the way he had spoken to her had put her to flight. She had left the party rather than stay to be tormented by him.

But now he was laid low, in bed, unable to go out into

12

the June sunshine, with no family to visit him. No Toni, either. On sudden impulse she went to the telephone dir-ectory, looked up the number of the hospital and dialled it. A cool hygienic voice informed her that there was a visiting hour that afternoon.

Soon she was on top of a red double-decker bus as it swayed eastwards. In one hand she clutched a bunch of roses, in the other she held a bag containing a cluster of purple grapes.

The bus stopped at the hospital gates and with several other people she alighted and followed them through an arched doorway into a big echoing entrance hall. At the information desk she was directed to the ward and then rode in a lift with other visitors who were also carrying flowers.

A plump West Indian nurse smiled brightly at her when she asked for Mr Mallon and took her to the bed nearest the window on the left. There was nothing on the bedside locker except a water jug and a glass; no flowers, no bowls of fruit, no boxes of chocolates, as there were on the lockers beside the other beds.

'Here's your girl-friend to see you, Mr Mallon,' said the nurse cheerfully, as she pulled out a screen made from cream curtains stretched across a tubular frame which moved on wheels and opened out.

The man lying on the bed turned his head quickly. There was a bandage round his head covering his eyes.

'Toni?' he queried.

Deirdre opened her mouth to speak, failed, and looked round wildly at the nurse who, noticing her discomfiture, whispered,

'He can't see yet.'

Blind! The word seemed to screech through Deirdre's mind as she looked down at the flowers in her hand. Of what use were they to a blind man? She looked at the nurse, who shrugged her shoulders and smiled sadly, took the flowers and tiptoed away round the edge of the screen.

'Toni?' His voice was as she remembered it, attractively

13

husky. 'Where are you?' he demanded.

'I . . . I'm Deirdre Lane,' she stammered. 'Toni couldn't come. She's sorry. Her flight schedules. . . .' Her voice faded away to silence. Unable to hide his disappointment, he had turned away from her, and all she could see was the rough brown hair spiking over the white bandage at the back of his head.

Moving carefully, she placed the bag of grapes on top of the locker and sat down in the chair the nurse had set beside the bed. The two screens, one at the foot of the bed and one between it and the next bed, made a small, oddly intimate room in which she was alone with a stranger who was wishing she was Toni.

From beyond the screen behind her came the sound of chatter and laughter as other patients enjoyed the company of their visitors. Not knowing what to do or say next Deirdre sat staring at Rory Mallon. One of his arms lay outside the bedclothes, the pushed-up sleeve of a blue-and-white striped pyjama jacket revealing a brawny forearm covered with brown hairs, a strong wrist and a hand hidden by bandages.

She could feel his disappointment almost as acutely as if it had been her own, so she sat there clutching her handbag, suffering with him. Suddenly her nose began to itch. She opened her handbag and took out a handkerchief, in case the antiseptic used in the hospital, and to which she was allergic, made her sneeze. The catch on the handbag closed with a sharp snapping sound. At once Rory turned his head and asked,

'You're still there?'

'Yes. I've brought you some grapes. I've brought you some flowers too, roses; you see, I didn't know. Toni didn't tell me that . . . that. . . .' For some reason her throat closed up and she could not say the word.

'That I'm blind,' he finished for her flatly.

Below the bandage his face was gaunt, thin with suffering. The high cheekbones looked dark and bruised, yet his mouth had the same ruthless curve that she remembered

14

and his chin, blurred by brown stubble, had a hard clean line.

'Are you permanently blind?' she asked tentatively.

'I hope not. It's a form of snow-blindness caused by severe exposure to the glare of the sun or snow. It may be weeks before I can see again. Weeks!' The husky voice cracked despairingly.

She remembered painfully that he was a photographer, and depended on his eyes; without sight he could not know if there was anything to photograph. This new and excruciating feeling she was experiencing must be empathy. Never before had she felt like this. It was as if her own personality had been projected into his so that she fully understood his misery and frustration. If only she had known him longer she could have shown how she felt by placing a hand on his arm. She knew that a touch can often convey much more than words.

'Perhaps I can help,' she offered diffidently.

'You? Why should you? I don't know you. What did you say your name is?'

The short rough sentences gave his questions a callousness which recalled the last time she had seen him, when he had been unkindly witty at her expense and drove out the feelings of compassion.

'Deirdre Lane. We met once, last September, at a party at Toni's flat.'

'I don't remember you,' his honesty was devastating, 'at least not by name. Remind me of how you look. I usually remember faces, especially women's faces.' Now there was a trace of amusement in his voice and she noticed that the line of his mouth had relaxed. She wished suddenly that she could make him smile or laugh.

'How can I remind you?' she asked.

'Describe yourself. It will help to pass the time. For both of us.' Amusement had gone, replaced by a bitter weariness, and she shifted uneasily on the chair as she tried to respond to his demand.

'Well, I'm dark,' she began selfconsciously.

15

'Swarthy?' he queried quickly, obviously not satisfied with her beginning.

'Oh, no. My hair, I mean. It's actually black and straight.'

'Short or long?'

'Long, just now.' How extraordinarily difficult it was to describe oneself.

'How long? Shoulder-length?'

'Almost to my waist.'

'That's a lot of hair.' He almost smiled. 'How do you wear it? Loose? Flowing freely?'

'No, I usually wind it up into a bun at the back of my neck.'

He grimaced his dislike.

'I don't like that style. What colour are your eyes?'

'A sort of greyish-green.'

'Sort of,' he jeered. 'Either they are or they're not. Do you have black eyelashes?'

'Yes, I do.'

'Long ones?'

'Well . . . er . . . yes. They are fairly long.' She found she could not help laughing.

'Good. I like the way you laugh. Makes me think of the sound of a mountain stream. What's your complexion like?'

'Pale.'

'Nose?'

'Amost straight.'

'Almost!' His exclamation was disgusted. 'What does that mean? Be more accurate. Has it got a hump in the middle or does it turn up at the end?'

'It turns up a little at the end.'

'What about your mouth? Would I like to kiss it?'

That silenced her, reminding her of the way he had behaved at that party of Toni's. Colour flamed into her face and she was glad he couldn't see it as she glanced at his mouth; there was a wicked curl at the corner of it. He knew he had embarrassed her.

'I don't know,' she replied coldly.

16

'There's one way I could find out,' he suggested.

'Now you're being impertinent,' she said sharply.

The curl at the corner of his mouth increased, developing into a downward curve.

'Impertinence is one of my vices, as you have reason to know. I remember you now—you're the prim and proper schoolteacher. You sat in a corner all evening looking down that nose of yours; you were shocked by the somewhat uninhibited behaviour of the rest of us.'

'I wasn't shocked,' she defended weakly.

'Of course you were! It was your first meeting with Toni's swinging friends and you didn't like any of us, but in particular you didn't like me. You left early and we had a good laugh about you after you'd gone,' he said callously. 'Why did you come here today?'

'Because Toni asked me,' she retorted stiffly. 'But if I'd known you were going to be rude and unpleasant I might have had second thoughts and not visited you.'

'Come off the high horse, love,' he countered with a sudden disarming grin, 'you knew already that I can be rude and unpleasant. *Deirdre*. You'd have thought I'd have remembered an outlandish name like that, wouldn't you? How did you get it? Irish, isn't it?'

'Yes. My mother came from Ireland,' she said, trying to subdue the anger which his careless mockery roused in her. 'She was interested in Celtic mythology and the story of Deirdre of the Sorrows was one of her favourites.'

'Never heard of it,' he said in a dismissing way. 'What do you teach.'

'History,' she answered shortly.

'Sounds dull. Where?'

'At a girls' grammar school.'

'I get the impression you're a bit above my touch. Are you going to be married?'

'No, I'm not. You're very curious.'

'Nothing else to do,' he muttered, turning his head restlessly on the pillow. Immediately she was annoyed with herself. She wasn't doing very well in her rôle as a visitor to

17

someone who was ill.

'Toni told me you were hurt when you fell in that accident in the Himalayas. It must have been. . . .' She broke off because he had turned his head again, and she could see that anguish had darkened his face. His mouth was a taut line of pain.

'I watched a friend die . . . slowly,' he said huskily. 'I wish I'd died with him.'

'Oh no, you mustn't say that!' She was suddenly horrified at what she had done. Thinking that talking about his ordeal might have helped him, she had reminded him of the tragic death of someone who had obviously been close to him and at the same time had reminded him of his own helplessness.

'Why mustn't I?' he demanded, his voice rising. 'What good am I if I can't see? I can't take photographs. I can't climb. I might as well be dead.'

One of the screens was pushed aside. The nurse appeared, an expression of disapproval on her normally benign face. She glared at Deirdre.

'Now, Mr Mallon, that's enough,' she ordered sharply. 'Remember what the doctor told you, you won't do yourself any good by getting worked up. It isn't any use fretting. I'll have to ask your visitor to leave.'

'Hell,' he muttered violently, turning away from them so that they couldn't see his face. Then he turned back quickly as he heard Deirdre getting to her feet. 'You'll come again tomorrow Deirdre, please?'

The desperation in his entreaty touched her. Although only a few minutes ago she had vowed to herself that she would never come again to see such a rude man, she agreed to visit him again and left the ward.

She visited him again the next day and then every evening of the following week. Each time he seemed better. They talked about everything, places they had both visited, people in the news, about anything but climbing and photography. She described the weather, the other patients, the nurses, the scene she could see beyond the window, and any

18

incidents which had happened to her during the day which had amused her; talking about anything which would distract him and take his mind off the plight which he seemed to find frustrating to such a great degree, probably because he had always lived life to the full.

'You're good, you know,' he said abruptly one evening.

'At what?'

'Description. You were slow to start, but now you've realised what I'm missing you make everything very clear to me. You should write.'

'What would I write about?' she asked with a laugh.

'What do women write about? You've studied history. Why not write historical romances?'

It was the first time he had shown any real interest in her personally since he had asked if she was married.

'I don't think I could write those,' she replied, 'I don't know anything about romance.'

'No lovers?' he queried.

'No, no lovers,' she said primly. 'When are they going to remove the bandages?'

'Tomorrow. Will you come again?'

She had intended to go down to see Aunt Irene and Uncle Bert, catching a train as soon as school had finished on Friday. But the intention was pushed aside as so many of her intentions had been pushed aside since she had started to visit Rory. He was fast becoming the most important person in her life, even though she was always warning herself that there was danger in letting him take over.

Days were passing by in a blur and she knew that her classes were noticing her absent-mindedness, her lack of interest in them, and were consequently playing up to get her attention. For the first time since she had started to teach she found her work dull, and the hours could not pass fast enough during the day as she looked forward to her evening visit to the hospital.

It was hard to believe that only a week had passed since she had met Toni, she thought as she caught the bus on

Friday evening. Although she had tried to contact her friend she had had no luck; even leaving a message with the airline at the airport had brought no response. She knew that Toni had not been in touch with Rory, because although he never mentioned her, the nurses had told her that no other woman had visited him.

She had taken some trouble with her appearance in case he could see; taking a tip from Toni she had bought a new blouse the colour of a spring leaf, and she had to admit that the fresh green did enhance the shade of her eyes and drew attention to her ivory-tinted skin.

Rory was sitting up in bed exchanging jokes with the man in the next bed, and looked tidier than on her previous visits. His hair had been brushed, he had been shaved, and under his thick slanting eyebrows she could see that his eyes were grey, the wild bluish-grey of the stormy sea.

'Can you see?' she asked, because he seemed to be looking right at her.

'Not properly. Only dim shapes. Would I like your shape, Deirdre?' he asked, with that now familiar taunting grin.

'I don't know,' she retorted coolly, and his grin widened.

'One day I'll find out,' he replied tantalisingly, leaning back against his pillows.

Without the bandages on his hands and round his head he seemed less vulnerable, and she realised with a jolt of pain that she knew very little about him. Now that he was growing stronger the possibility of his leaving hospital was looming large, so that the chances of getting to know him better were growing slimmer and slimmer. Once he had left he would go back to that other world of his; a world of fashion models and wealthy clients where she had no entry.

'I had a letter today,' he announced, 'I'd like you to read it to me, please. It's in the drawer of the bedside locker.'

She opened the drawer and drew out the thick white envelope. At once she recognised the sloping writing; it was from Toni. She told him, and he ordered her to open it and read it.

There was a single sheet of paper in the envelope and the message was brief, and to her relief, unsentimental.

'Dear Rory,' she read. 'I feel terrible because I haven't been able to visit you this week. Hope Deirdre has been able to fill in. I shall come on Saturday as I have something very important to tell you. Love from Toni.'

Deirdre folded the piece of paper and placed it in the envelope. Reading it had not been as difficult as she had anticipated, and now she knew she wouldn't have to visit him tomorrow. She would be able to go down to Berkshire with a clear conscience.

'You have a beautiful voice,' he said suddenly. 'I wish I could see you properly . . . in colour.'

'You'll be glad that Toni is coming tomorrow,' she said with a sharp cheerfulness, trying to ignore the strange shaking which his comment had caused within her. 'It's just as well she's coming, because I won't be able to visit you tomorrow or on Sunday.'

'Why not?' He'd turned his head and again she felt he could see her. The blank stare of his unfocussed eyes was unnerving.

'I have to go to Berkshire, to the church in the town where I used to live.'

'Why?' he demanded rather irritably, and the inner shaking transferred itself to her fingers as she pulled open the drawer of the locker and put Toni's letter in it. Was he irritable because her visits had begun to mean as much to him as they had to her? No, that couldn't be. That was romancing, and she mustn't indulge in that.

'I have to go and lay a wreath on my parents' grave—it's the third anniversary of their death. They were killed in an accident,' she murmured.

'What sort of an accident?'

'A plane crash. They'd been to Jerusalem and were on their way back. My father was a Doctor of Divinity and had taken a party of students from the theological college, where he lectured, to visit the Holy City.'

'A teacher of religion for a father. Perhaps that's why

21

you're so moral,' he teased.

'The way I think about some things has nothing to do with what my father did for a living,' she retorted.

'What things?'

'How to behave towards other people, knowing the difference between right and wrong,' she answered carefully, not wanting to give him any chance to mock her as he had at Toni's party.

'But you think I have no morals at all,' he accused so suddenly that she actually drew away from the bed.

'No, no ... I've never said that, I don't think that,' she denied hurriedly. 'But I do think you like to shock people deliberately by doing something unexpected or by behaving unconventionally.'

His grin was taunting and she braced herself for the mockery which, she realised now, was bound to come.

'My, my, we are being diplomatic tonight, aren't we?' he jeered. 'So I do the unexpected and behave unconventionally? By your standards, possibly, but not by mine. I admit my actions are governed by self-interest, but then I've only myself to please and it's been that way all my life. I haven't had any parents breathing down my neck insisting that I conform.'

'Yes, Toni told me you haven't any family,' she murmured.

'And you'd like me to tell you why I haven't, wouldn't you?' he jibed. 'Well, there's nothing to tell.'

'I see. Then could you tell me why you like to climb mountains?' She refused to be stopped in her determination to learn more about him.

'To get to the top of them, of course,' he mocked.

'Oh, if you won't tell me anything about yourself how can you expect me to understand you?' she flared, suddenly irritated by his deliberate evasion of her questions.

'Do you want to understand me?' He sounded surprised.

'Yes, I do. I want to know why you went on that expedition.'

'To fulfil an ambition. To photograph the mountains. I

22

took four cameras and enough film for three thousand exposures.' He paused, his mouth tightening. 'I used most of it and it's all waiting to be developed. Do you know anything about developing film, Deirdre?'

'A little, I've always developed my own snapshots. You must have done some mountaineering before the expedition or you wouldn't have been invited to go on it,' she persisted.

'Right again. Mountaineering has been my form of recreation ever since I was in my teens. I grew up in a big city, and to escape from it I used to go with friends into the countryside at the weekends. We were a gang of toughs out to climb anything we could in any way we could.' A gleam of amusement chased across the hollows and angles of his face. 'Never mind following the rules and regulations laid down by the climbing clubs, we were going to get to the top even if we were killed doing it. It was a crazy, exhilarating time of my life, but you wouldn't have liked me then, Deirdre.'

She glanced quickly at him. He had closed his eyes as if he were tired of trying to see, and she stared at his bruised face and at the big scarred hands resting in the white bedcover, and her heart seemed to twist painfully. His daring, his need to pit himself against great odds, had brought him to this.

'What makes you think I like you now?' she retorted defensively. The line of his mouth softened as he smiled.

'You're here. You've come every night for a week.'

'Because Toni asked me to,' she hedged.

'And do you always do what Toni asks you?' he teased.

'No ... I mean .. yes,' she said in confusion, and he laughed. Her cheeks flamed and she asked hurriedly, 'Which came first, the climbing or the photography?'

'Question period continues,' he jeered. 'You sound just like an interviewer on the radio or the television. Does it matter which came first?'

'No, I suppose it doesn't. I should have asked why did you go in for photography?'

'That's better,' he mocked. 'When I left school I went to work for a company which made photographic equipment. Not an exciting job, just the boy who fetched and carried. It kept me off the streets and earned me a few pounds.' The twist to his mouth was wry as he made fun of himself. 'Unlike you, I wasn't studious; in fact I hated school.'

'I can imagine,' she murmured drily.

'Almost against my will I became interested in cameras and what could be done with them. I borrowed a good one and took it with me when I went climbing. I photographed the beauty which I saw and discovered I had a talent. Suddenly I wanted to climb the greats, the Alps and the Himalayas, and photograph them. Ambition was born where there had been none.'

He paused and rubbed at his face with one hand, then continued more slowly.

'It wasn't as easy to fulfil as I'd imagined, but something happened which made me realise that with my background, or lack of it, no one was going to invite me to go on a mountaineering expedition. And I had no money to finance my own.'

'So what did you do?'

'Rebelled. I bought a camera, came to London and talked my way into a job photographing fashion models for magazines. I met a model who was as ambitious to be known and to make money as I was, and in a few years I had well-known people queueing up to have their photograph taken by *me*.' His mouth curved cynically. 'And I could afford to freelane. At last I could climb those other mountains and photograph them.'

Deirdre pushed the chair back and stood up. He heard her movements and sat up straight.

'Is it that time already?' he asked. 'Will you come again next week?'

'I ... I'm afraid I can't. I have to prepare papers for summer exams,' she replied, her throat suddenly dry. 'Anyway, you'll have Toni. She'll be pleased to see you looking so much better.'

24

'Will she?' he said drily. 'Don't leave yet. I want to ask you something.'

'I must go, Rory. I have to catch a train. I expect we'll meet again some time—perhaps at Toni's. Goodbye.'

'Deirdre, will you wait?' he roared suddenly.

She didn't wait. She turned and fled unseeingly, almost bumping into a nurse who was coming to see what was the matter with Mr Mallon this time, aware that everyone in the ward had stopped talking to stare in amazement at her hasty departure. Along the corridor she hurried to the stairs, not bothering with the lift in case there was someone in it who might see the tears which were spattering her cheeks.

CHAPTER TWO

As the electric train rushed through the gathering twilight on its way into Berkshire, Deirdre faced up to reality. Her sudden decision not to visit Rory any more, her swift flight from his bedside, had not been based on reason, she realised, but were the result of an instinctive withdrawal from the precipice which had opened unexpectedly at her feet, and into which she had almost fallen headlong.

It was Toni's letter which had sounded the bell of warning. The letter had come just in time to remind her that Rory and Toni had an arrangement; for a few days she had been foolish enough to forget that arrangement. She had allowed her compassion for Rory's present state of blindness to lead her into a world which had been so far unknown to her, but to which she had often longed to be invited; the world of romance.

The truth was painful. When Rory left hospital he and Toni would take up their arrangement again, she was sure of that. With his attitude towards convention, particularly towards marriage, he probably found that the arrangement suited him very well—he would never give Deirdre another thought once he was with Toni again. She had been useful for a while and had relieved his boredom, but that was all. Yes, it would be safer not to visit him again.

So she made every effort to wipe him from her mind during the next few weeks, involving herself fully in her work and in preparations for the holidays, planning to go to Spain and not to Scotland.

Returning to the flat one day feeling exhausted, she dropped her briefcase on the nearest chair and flopped down on the settee, kicking off her shoes to ease her feet. The weather was warm and sultry after a few days of high temperatures, and there was a threat of thunder in the big cauliflower-like clouds which had been building up all afternoon and now obscured the sun.

'You look whacked,' said Elise Downie as she crossed the room and set down a cup of tea on the small table near the settee. 'Why so late, Dee?'

'Staff meeting. I thought the Crab would never stop droning on and on about the arrangements for sports day,' replied Deirdre. "The Crab" was the usual nickname for Miss Hermit, the headmistress of the school where she taught. 'This tea tastes good—remind me to do the same for you one day.'

'Don't worry, I will,' retorted Elise, a smile curving her determined rosebud-pink mouth. She was a small, thin girl with a pretty pink-and-white face framed by curving brown hair. Behind big round glasses her blue eyes had an innocent look, but her apparent demureness hid a cool analytical mind which Deirdre often envied. Elise taught mathematics, and made no secret of the fact that she was ambitious. She had little time for romance and was an active supporter of the Women's Rights movement.

'I hope you haven't forgotten that we're going over to Daphne's place to make final arrangements for going to Spain,' she said now, her glance roving over Deirdre.

26

'No, I hadn't forgotten, but would you mind going with-out me? I feel very tired. You could tell them what I think and come to some conclusion.'

Elise frowned.

'You're not really interested in going to Spain, are you?' she said shrewdly. 'You couldn't care less where you go for your holidays. In fact you're not interested in anything, and you're all white and dark-eyed like a tragic heroine. If you asked me, I'd say you're heading for a nervous breakdown.'

'Teacher's complaint,' murmured Deirdre, closing her eyes. She couldn't face getting into an argument with Elise just now. If only she could sink into a long dreamless sleep, and forget this awful feeling of guilt.

'That's a lot of nonsense,' retorted Elise crisply, 'I don't believe you would let a class of teenagers get you down. It's something else. You're worried about something—or is it someone? Wouldn't it help to tell me, Dee?'

Deirdre opened her eyes and studied the pretty face which was lit by inquisitive blue eyes. No, she couldn't tell. Elise wouldn't understand how anyone could miss the com-pany of a man after having known him for only one hour a day for a week. So she didn't reply, and picking up the cup she finished her tea.

'All right, I can take a hint,' sighed Elise, 'no true con-fession is forthcoming tonight. By the way, someone rang up about half an hour ago; left his number but not his name. I've written the number on the pad by the phone. He wants you to ring him as soon as you come in. I'll go and finish getting the meal ready.'

She went out. Deirdre waited until the door had closed, then slid off the settee and went over to the phone. The number scrawled on the pad was a local one, and at the sight of it her heart began to pound with excitement. Only one man she knew lived in the area covered by that code.

Quickly she dialled the number and waited for someone to answer while all sorts of thoughts tumbled through her mind. At last there was the sound of a receiver being lifted, and a familiar husky voice spoke.

27

'Hello.'

'Rory? This is Deirdre. Where are you?'

'At my studio, down by the river.'

'When did you leave hospital?'

'A few weeks ago. I've been in a convalescent place since then. I came here two days ago.'

'Can you see?' Her voice was full of anxiety.

'A little,' he responded uncommunicatively.

'Then how are you managing to look after yourself?'

'Not badly. Mrs Dobson who has always cleaned this place for me, helps by making my meals, and a few of my friends blow in now and again. Will you come to see me?'

'When?' Deirdre was startled.

'Now.'

'I ... I ... don't think I can. I'm going out with some friends.'

'Drop'em and come here instead. If you don't come....' He stopped speaking abruptly and she asked anxiously,

'Rory? Are you still there?'

'Yes, I'm still here, but if you don't come tonight I won't be responsible for what I might do next. Imagine the headline in tomorrow's papers: Well-known photographer found lying....'

'Stop it!' she shrieked into the mouthpiece, and then heard him laugh.

'I thought that would touch your Celtic soul. You'll come here now, please, Deirdre?'

This time she thought she heard a note of desperation in his voice and all her defences came crumbling down.

'Yes, I'll come. Give me the address.'

He gave it to her and added that she would find the front door open so she could walk right in. Then he rang off. She left at once, ignoring Elise's complaints about her letting down Daphne and Susan, refusing even to stay and eat. She went by taxi, arriving outside an old brick building which faced the slow grey river just as lightning crackled across the sky, thunder rumbled and the heavens opened to pour out slanting silvery rain.

The building had once been a small warehouse. The brickwork had been re-pointed, new windows had been set into it and their frames and the front door painted a pale Wedgwood blue. Inside the door was a store-room with a concrete floor, and to the right an open staircase led up to the next floor.

She stood hesitantly, hearing the rain swishing down outside and wondering where she should look for Rory.

'Won't you come into my parlour, said the spider to the fly?' His voice mocked her from above. He was standing at the top of the stairs, and in the storm light he seemed bigger than she remembered.

Thunder crashed as she went slowly up the stairs, her eyes sliding sideways to the photographs on the walls. Photographs of mountains shining under sunlight, glowering under clouds; pinnacles of sharp rock soaring against brilliantly blue skies; precipices yawning blackly.

When she reached the top of the stairs Rory had gone, and she turned to find herself, not on a landing with doors opening on to it, but another big room, the floor covered with black-and-white carpeting. Huge blown-up photographs of living things—parts of human faces, branches of trees, petals of flowers, wings of birds, covered the walls. Against one wall hung drawn-back black draperies which presumably divided the space into two when they were drawn across.

In one half of the room several spotlights and cameras, all on tripods, were collected together with other photographic equipment. In the other half, near two long windows facing the river, were several long settees covered in white leather trimmed with black, some armchairs and occasional tables. Rory was standing beside the cocktail bar with a glass in his hand. He seemed to be looking at her, and she guessed he knew she was there because he could hear her moving.

'Come over here,' he said. 'I'm afraid you'll have to pour your own drink—I've tried once and made a hopeless mess. Spilt the stuff. Can you smell it?'

On the bar there was a collection of bottles and glasses. Deirdre sniffed.

'Yes, I can smell it, but I don't want anything. I don't drink.'

'Well, perhaps you'd pour something for me. Whisky, please,' he said.

'Do you think you should?' she ventured. 'I mean, is it wise to drink when you can't see?'

'If you're going to preach, love, you can go back where you came from,' he jibed.

She looked closely at him. Dark glasses concealed his eyes and made him look mysterious and somehow alien, and the high rolled collar of his white sweater emphasized the angularity of his lean face. Although he was clean-shaven his hair needed trimming, and it was ruffled as if he had been running his fingers through it. There was about him a tenseness which indicated that he was in a dangerous mood.

'Very well,' she murmured, taking the glass from him and pouring some liquor into it, 'there you are. Have you eaten today?'

'Not since midday. Mrs Dobson said she'd left a casserole of chicken for me to warm up, but I didn't feel like it.'

I haven't eaten either,' she said, suddenly knowing what to do to distract him. 'Do you mind if I share your supper?'

'Not if you don't mind getting it ready.'

'Do you have a kitchen?' she asked.

'Yes, through the door in the corner of this room. That leads to the kitchen-cum-dining room; the other door leads to the dark rooms. Bathroom and bedrooms are up that flight of stairs in the other corner.'

'You seem to be moving about without any trouble,' she observed as he followed her into the bright well-equipped kitchen.

'That's because I know where everything is here. I haven't found the courage to go outside yet.' He paused, then added rather savagely, 'Being blind is like being in prison, only there's no way of escape.'

Taking off her coat, Deirdre threw it over the back of a chair. All her compassion for him roused as she began to prepare a meal, searching for and finding the casserole of chicken, putting it in the oven to warm up, finding rice and vegetables to cook, setting the table. While she worked Rory leaned against a wall and sipped his whisky and they talked. There was no restraint between them; it was as if they had been meeting every day for the past few weeks instead of having no contact at all.

'Why were you so late getting home?' he asked eventually.

'Staff meeting. There's always so much to do at the end of term.'

'When does the term end?'

'Next Thursday, at noon.'

'Going away for your holidays?' he asked idly.

'Yes. With Elise and a couple of other friends.'

'All females?'

'Yes. We're touring Spain by car.' Deirdre's voice was calm.

'How exciting,' he jeered. She was nettled by his tone.

'I wanted to go to Scotland, but the others wouldn't agree.'

'You could go there with me,' he said quietly. She turned to glance at him, but his face was unreadable.

'The meal's ready now.' She decided to ignore his remark.

'If you look in the fridge you'll find a bottle of white wine,' he said.

'It isn't necessary,' she answered.

'Not for you perhaps, my puritan, but I'd like some. You'll find glasses in the top left-hand cupboard.'

When they were sitting down at the table she asked him about his sight.

'There's still hope,' he answered. 'It's taking its time, though, and I'm not the most patient of men. The specialist recommended that I should go away and relax, forget about it, and it'll return as my health improves. I've made some

31

arrangements.'

As usual he made no mention of Toni, and Deirdre could only assume that her friend was part of his arrangements.

'Where are you going?' she asked.

'To Scotland; the island of Jura, to be exact. I have a cottage there. All I need now is someone to go with me, a companion who could do the cooking and housekeeping and who could also help me select photographs and other information for a book I've been asked to prepare about the expedition. Someone who knows how to write. I thought of you,' he said casually. 'How would you like to come with me to Jura for the rest of the summer, instead of going to Spain?'

Surprise kept her silent for a few seconds. She sat watching him eat and drink, marvelling at the accuracy with which he could do both.

'What about Toni?' she said at last.

He placed his knife and fork together and picked up his wine glass. Above it she saw her own reflection in his dark glasses,

'Toni isn't interested in living with a half-blind man,' he said colly, and raising his glass to his lips he drained it.

'I'm sorry,' she mumbled inadequately. What else could she say?

He ignored her sympathy and leaned back in his chair.

'Well, what do you think? Will you come to Jura with me?' he asked.

How difficult it was to assess the sincerity of a person when you couldn't see the expression in his eyes. How impossible to guess at the motives lying behind his invitation.

'I couldn't live with you, Rory, if that's what you want,' she said quickly, taking a chance.

'That's what I want,' he answered just as quickly. 'Could you if we were married?'

She was shaken, because the question was the very last she had expected from him.

'Don't mock,' she rebuked him in a low voice. 'You don't

mean what you've just said.'

'I'm not in the habit of saying what I don't mean,' he retorted. 'I've had plenty of time to think it over and I've decided that if it's the only way I can get you to come to Jura with me for the summer, I'll marry you.'

'But we hardly know each other,' she countered wildly.

'I disagree; I think we know each other quite well. I know enough about you to realise you wouldn't come unless the realtionship is all legal and above board. I also know you have abilities which in my present state of helplessness I can use. Tonight I've learned that you're not a bad cook— there are two other things I need to know about you. Can you type, and can you drive a car?'

'Yes, I can, but you don't marry a woman only because she has abilities you can use,' she objected. 'There's more to marriage than that.'

'I'm glad you realise that,' he murmured drily. 'Losing my sight at this time in my life is damned inconvenient—I need help and you can help me. I know it sounds selfish and unromantic, but I can't put it any other way.' He paused, then added very quietly, 'There's no one else I can ask, and if you won't agree I don't know what I'm going to do. Go crazy, I expect.'

Deirdre was silent again, a prey to conflicting emotions. The lack of romance in his approach hurt her, but on the other hand she understood why he had asked her. Being blind, for however short a time, was depriving him of his freedom. He was like a caged hawk, searching for a way of making his imprisonment endurable. She could help him to find that way. It was something which appealed to her compassionate nature.

Bothered by her continuing silence, he moved restlessly, and stood up so suddenly that his chair toppled over backwards to crash noisily to the floor. Startled out of her musings, Deirdre sprang to her feet, but as she moved he moved too, and they bumped into each other. At once he grasped her by the arms.

'Where are you going?' he demanded.

33

'To pick up the chair.'

'Leave it and we'll go and sit more comfortably in the other room.'

He slid a hand down her arm to take her hand. Feeling his way with his other hand, he led her out of the kitchen into the big studio room; the storm had passed and wan sunlight slanted in through the long windows.

They sat side by side on one of the settees, and Rory said rather wearily,

'I believe the ball is in your court. Aren't you going to lob it back?'

The absence of any sentiment in his proposal made it seem cold and brutal, yet she was glad he was honest about it. He wouldn't be proposing to her if he wasn't blind—he wouldn't be proposing if Toni hadn't let him down in his hour of need. He was turning to her, the next woman, guessing accurately at her compassion for him in his present state, hoping she might be persuaded to be his summer wife.

'Deirdre,' he prompted softly.

'Do I have to give you an answer now?' she asked, thinking she should ask advice before committing herself.

'Now.' His tone was relentless.

'I'll have to tell Aunt Irene and Uncle Bert,' she said.

'That's your affair,' he replied curtly.

'I'd like them to meet you. . . .'

'No.' He spoke vehemently.

'But why not? They're very gentle people, they'll understand about your not being able to see. There's no need for you to be shy.'

'I'm not exactly the shy type,' he said with a grin, 'but the answer is still no. I took that sort of test once and failed it.'

'What sort of test? I don't understand.'

'I don't expect you to. I've reached an age when I don't have to explain myself to anyone or take any tests, means or otherwise. I can afford to keep you in relative comfort, and although I wasn't brought up in the same way as you've been, I shan't beat you,' he added with a touch of bitterness.

'Oh, they wouldn't be looking for ways to prevent me from marrying you!' she exclaimed. 'They aren't my parents, just two people I'm very fond of and who'll be hurt if I don't tell them.'

'Tell them if you want to, but let's get this straight before we go any further,' he said tersely, 'this is between you and me, and has nothing to do with anyone else. The fewer people involved the better. Then, if later we decide to call it quits when my sight has come back, no one is upset or disturbed. There'll be no presents, no guests, just a simple civil contract signed by you and me before a couple of witnesses and the Registrar. We do it that way or not at all.'

The independent woman in her, who disliked being dominated, reacted against his autocratic manner and showed in her sharp answer.

'Would you mind telling me when you'd like me to sign the contract? The date might not be convenient for me.'

'Next Thursday, when you've finished school. That night we'll put the car on the overnight train to Glasgow, and next morning we'll drive to Tarbert to catch the ferry to the island. We should be in the cottage by four o'clock.'

He was going too fast for Deirdre. She felt as if a tidal wave had overtaken her and was sweeping her to an unknown shore. Desperately she clutched at any straw which might slow down that impetuous rush.

'But my job. What about my job?' It came out as a last despairing cry.

'What about it?'

'I can't give notice now, it's too late. It has to be given three months beforehand, according to my contract. I'll have to go back in September.'

Rory laughed, and stretched his arms along the back of the settee. One of his hands touched her head and his fingers explored what they had found, sliding down to touch her neck, to stroke the line of her chin. A strange shudder went through her body as every nerve of her body

35

resented the careless yet experienced caress. It was the first time any man had ever touched her in such a way.

'Anyone could guess you're not used to being a rebel,' he scoffed softly, 'you're too concerned about what other people might think if you do something which is a little out of line. You know, by September I might be able to see properly again, and by then you might be so heartily sick of me you'll be glad to have a job to come back to. In my experience nothing ever lasts, and this marriage of ours might only last the summer. Well, what do you say? Yes or no?'

In spite of his casual manner she sensed his desperation. If she didn't agree to marry him and go with him to Jura, what would happen to him? She could easily imagine him going berserk as he fretted against his temporary imprisonment.

'Yes,' she said quickly before she could change her mind, 'I'll marry you—for better or for worse.'

'It'll probably be the worse for you,' he mocked. 'Thanks, love, that's a load off my mind. Now give me your hand.'

She placed her hand in the one he held out to her. His fingers gripped hard and then explored.

'A big hand for a woman. It feels capable, though,' he murmured. 'I'd like you to make a promise, Deirdre.'

'What is it?'

'It's not easy to explain. I realise that what we're going to do is for my convenience more than anything else, and I feel I have to offer you something else other than your keep and a holiday in Scotland. So I want you to promise to tell me if you meet someone you'd prefer to be married to before the summer is over and I'll let you go.'

'You mean if I fall madly in love with another man, I've to tell you and our marriage will end?' She spoke as lightly as she could.

'That's it.'

'It's a strange promise to make before we ever get married,' she protested. 'Marriage is supposed to be for ever.'

36

He was silent for a moment, eyebrows slanting in a frown.

'I know you believe that,' he said at last, 'I'm just trying to avoid complications. We can only do that if we promise to be completely honest with each other. It could happen—you could fall in love, as you call it.'

'So could you,' she countered. 'I'll only make a promise like that if you'll do the same.'

Again he was silent and frowning, as if he were uncertain how to proceed.

'It won't be fair if I promise to be honest and you don't, Rory,' she said softly.

'All right. I promise,' he replied quietly, and rather reluctantly she thought.

Later the same evening Deirdre told Elise that she was going to be married the following Thursday, and asked her to be a witness at the ceremony. Both in their nightwear, curled up in their favourite chairs, they were sipping their bedtime drinks—hot chocolate for Deirdre and lemon juice for Elise—and discussing the day's major events, something they had done ever since they decided to share a flat.

Elise's wise yet curiously innocent eyes widened behind the big lenses of her spectacles.

'You're joking!' she exclaimed.

Deirdre shook her head, unable to control the small secret sense of triumph she felt at having surprised the usually unflappable Elise.

'No. Why should I joke about it?' she countered.

'Then you're out of your mind,' said Elise flatly.

'Why am I?' laughed Deirdre. 'People get married all the time, and no one suspects their sanity.'

'But you, of all people! and in a rush like this to a man you scarcely know! It's incredible! A person with brains and ability willingly submitting to the demands of a man as if you were his slave.' Elise's face was quite pink, and her eyes flashed.

'But I'm not submitting,' argued Deirdre, suddenly annoyed with her friend's superior and patronising manner. 'He needs help, and I've agreed to help him in the same way I'd help you if you needed it. I've chosen to do this freely.'

'Ha! He needs help now, but what about later, when his sight comes back? Will he need your help then, I wonder?' scoffed Elise.

'We've made a promise that if either of us wants our freedom later the marriage will end. We'll behave in a civilised manner,' replied Deirdre coolly.

Elise groaned, and rolled her eyes in disgust.

'A blind promise! Very appropriate in the circumstances,' she jeered, 'and easy to make now while neither of you is emotionally involved. Or *are* you emotionally involved, Dee?'

'I'm sorry for him,' said Deirdre slowly, 'I suppose that could count as being emotionally involved. Also he's been let down by a friend of mine at a time when he most needs help, and I feel responsible.'

'Oh, Dee, when will you learn?' groaned Elise. 'You go rushing in. You're a fool, not an angel, and he's just not worth it! No man is.'

'How do you know?' retorted Deirdre. 'You've not met him. He's an extremely talented person.'

'I grant you that, I've been to his exhibitions. I've read the reviews of them. A second Cartier-Bresson, one reviewer called him, able to capture the humour and pathos of life with the click of his camera. An artist of the highest calibre, another said. But think of his beginnings, Dee.'

'I didn't realise you were a snob,' said Deirdre stiffly. 'No one can help their beginnings.'

'I didn't mean it that way, I meant his beginnings as a photographer. Those pictures of fashion models. They're sheer exploitation of the female sex,' replied Elise, looking very severe and schoolmarmish. Deirdre stared at her in surprise, then burst out laughing.

'You're so funny,' she gasped. 'Haven't you realised those models wanted to be photographed in that way?

38

You're letting that propaganda about women's rights cloud your judgement.'

'I'm trying to make you see the man as he really is,' retorted Elise, her equanimity ruffled by Deirdre's criticism. 'Can't you see he's playing on your pity for him?'

'All I can see is that he needs someone like me at this time.'

'But what good is it going to do you? What are you going to get out of it?' demanded Elise, wholly exasperated because for once she wasn't winning an argument.

'Who knows? Maybe like Deirdre of the Sorrows, I'll get the richest and the best. Certainly I'll get a holiday in Scotland—you wouldn't go there with me, so I've found someone else.' Deirdre felt a sudden surge of gaiety. 'But you'll be a witness next Thursday, won't you, please? You won't feel you're being exploited if you do that for me?'

'I suppose so,' Elise agreed reluctantly. 'I'll help to lead the lamb to the slaughter. But don't come running to me afterwards for sympathy if it goes wrong for you.'

'I won't. Do you think you can find anyone to take my place on the trip to Spain?'

'I think so. Brenda Beach was saying only the other day that she wished there was room for her. Have you thought what you're going to say to the Crab? You'll have to tell her, you know.'

'I know, and it isn't going to be easy,' sighed Deirdre.

She told Miss Hermit the next day. The headmistress, a stylishly-dressed woman in her late forties, raised her eyebrows and stared at the youngest member of her staff. Returning that cool assessing gaze, Deirdre felt an unusual flare of rebellion. She knew the views of the Crab on marriage and her poor opinion of young women who allowed themselves to be trapped into it when they had alternatives such as well-paid jobs, and she often wondered why the woman was so sour about it. Was it possible that she had once suffered from unrequieted love?

'This is very sudden, Miss Lane, and not at all what I had expected from someone with your qualifications and ability,' drawled Miss Hermit in her thin, rather tired-sounding voice. 'Anyone can get married, you know.'

Deirdre tightened her lips to stop herself from retorting; she had learned earlier in the year that it was useless to offer her own point of view to Miss Hermit. As far as the headmistress was concerned there was only one point of view that was right—her own.

'You realise, I hope, that there is no possibility of you being released from your position here at such short notice,' Miss Hermit continued coldly.

'I've no wish to be released,' replied Deirdre tonelessly.

'No?' The expression on the headmistress's face was one of supercilious surprise.' I suppose that's something which can be said in your favour, although in my experience married women do not make the most reliable members of staff.' She smiled in a wintry way. 'They suffer from divided loyalties. However, I shall expect you back in September.'

Feeling frozen, Deirdre left the room, wondering why she now felt that by marrying Rory she was committing a sin.

At the weekend she went down to stay with her aunt and uncle, and once again she ran into disapproval; not of what she was going to do, but of the way she was going to do it. Aunt Irene, her father's sister, was a kindly woman who loved weddings. She was most put out when told that not only would there be no big wedding but that she was not invited to attend the simple ceremony in London.

'But, Deirdre, a summer wedding can be so lovely,' she said rather tearfully, 'and I feel that for your dear father's sake I should insist that you are married properly.'

'But I shall be married properly,' said Deirdre for the umpteenth time. She was beginning to feel rather limp—as Rory had commented, she was not used to being a rebel and overturning the authority to which she had submitted all her life. 'There isn't time to arrange it differently, and besides, Rory doesn't want to be married in church.'

To her great relief her uncle came to her rescue when all

40

her own arguments had failed to convince her aunt.

'Look at it this way, Irene,' he said patiently, 'this chap Rory is blind, so it's too much to expect him to go through the strain of a big wedding. I think he and Deirdre are going about it in the right way, considering what he's been through recently. We ought to be thankful that they're getting married and wish them good luck and God bless, instead of finding ways of making it difficult for them.'

Although Irene was still a little tearful, her husband's intervention put an end to further argument and the rest of Deirdre's stay in Berkshire passed pleasantly.

But the feeling that by marrying Rory she was taking a step which would cut her off from all the people she had ever known increased as the days rushed by. The thought of Toni bothered her, and several times she tried to get in touch with her friend without any luck. It was not until the night before the last day of term that she managed to talk to Toni's flat-mate over the phone.

'Oh, but didn't you know?' asked the drawling voice on the other end of the line. 'Toni's done it at last.'

'Done what?' Deirdre enquired blankly.

'She's caught a wealthy American! She's left the airline and gone to Paris with him—I wouldn't be a bit surprised if she has married him by now. I know that was what she was after.'

Thanking the woman for the information, Deirdre rang off. Now she knew what Toni had meant when she had said she was hoping to change her job and give up being an air hostess. And now she knew why Rory had been let down by her friend.

All her feelings for Rory seemed to rush together to form a determined purpose which overrode any doubts she had had about marrying him. She would make up to him for Toni's treatment of him in every way she could!

End-of-term activities at school and preparations for going to Scotland kept her occupied right up to the last minute. Thursday came, school finished and she returned to the flat to finish her packing, then in the late afternoon she

41

and Elise went to the Registrar's office in their district to meet Rory and his friend Dick Hunter, who was the other witness.

After the brief businesslike ceremony they all went in Rory's car back to his studio, where they had a meal which Deirdre prepared herself. Soon afterwards Elise left, and Dick helped Deirdre to finish packing the equipment for the writing of the book into the boot of the expensive, fast grey car.

Dick had been the leader of Rory's climbing expedition, a tall fair man with a bland, good-humoured face and sharp shrewd eyes. His attitude to Deirdre was cool and critical, and it dawned on her for the first time that Rory might have friends who considered it was he who was making the mistake by marrying her in a hurry, and not the other way round.

The impression that Dick felt like that was increased when, after driving them to the station and seeing to all the details of getting the car on the train and finding the right sleeping compartment for them, he turned to her and said coldly,

'Do you think you can manage now?'

'Yes, thank you,' she replied stiffly. They had left Rory in the compartment and walked along the corridor of the carriage to the door. Dick stepped down on to the platform, and Deirdre closed the door and let down the window to lean out.

'You can stop worrying about him,' she said, 'I've travelled by train before. I don't lose tickets or luggage and I can usually find my way back to the compartment if I have to leave it for any reason. I'm also a good driver, and I won't crash the car.'

Dick flushed uncomfortably.

'Sorry if I sounded a bit patronising,' he apologised. 'This whole business has left me gasping, and I'm wondering if Rory knows what he's done in marrying someone like you.'

'You're not very complimentary,' she retorted, and to her

amazement he swore with embarrassment and exasperation.

'Dammit, I didn't mean that. What I'm trying to say is, he may be blind, but he hasn't changed in any other way. He's a tough, ruthless realist—he wouldn't have survived that fall on the mountainside if he wasn't—and . . . oh, hell, there's no other way I can put it . . . he's not in love with you.'

'I know that,' she said quietly, feeling herself going cold and pale. It had been one thing to suspect that Rory was not in love with her but quite another to hear that thought expressed by a friend of his.

Dick looked surprisingly relieved and actually smiled at her.

'Do you?' he queried. 'That's all right, then. You won't be expecting too much from him. Sometimes women get funny ideas, and then they feel let down when a man doesn't live up to those ideas. I'll be off now.' He hesitated, then added, 'I'll be going up to Scotland later to do some climbing—Rory has suggested I cross over to Jura to see you.'

'I'll be pleased to welcome you when you come,' she said rather shyly. 'I expect you'll want to know when Rory's sight returns.'

He considered her narrowly for a few seconds, then to her surprise reached up and patted her hand where it rested on the lowered window.

'You'll do. I'll look forward to seeing you again. Good luck!' Deirdre didn't sleep well in the close confinement of the sleeping compartment as the train rushed through the dark countryside: several times she experienced near-panic as she realised what she had done. She had taken what she had always considered to be the most serious step any woman could take. She had married the man she could hear turning restlessly on the other bunk, a man she had disliked heartily when she had first met him; yet he had been able to draw her into that strangest of relationships, a marriage without love.

CHAPTER THREE

In spite of the fine drizzle which drenched the streets of Glasgow the next morning and in spite of the almost sleepless night she had spent aboard the train, Deirdre felt the usual upsurge of excitement that every new day brought to her. And today, the first day of her summer marriage, the excitement had a deliciously dangerous edge to it. An adventure was beginning.

As she drove the high-powered car away from the station along a main thoroughfare dim and dismal in the early morning rain, past the University and out along the Dumbarton Road, she sensed that Rory was nervous; he could not see where they were going and possibly he thought she might make a mess of driving his car. So she drove carefully, and gradually he leaned back and relaxed and began to answer the questions she asked him about the places they passed.

The road dipped close to the River Clyde where it widened out near Dumbarton, and the water looked smooth and sullen beneath the lowering clouds. But as they turned north, still following the coast to Helensburgh, the clouds lifted a little and she was able to see the bulk of green hills at the head of Loch Long. Soon she was driving beside the long narrow finger of the loch where it pointed inland to the village of Arrochar, a cluster of houses crouched under the rugged ramparts of the hills.

The roa dtwisted left, climbing through narrow passes, then turned south again to follow another loch which Rory told her was Loch Fyne.

At Ardrishaig they had to wait for the bridge over the entrance to the Crinan Canal to open while a 'uffer', one of the small coal-carrying boats which still take cargo to the outlying Hebridean Islands, passed into the lock. Deirdre made Rory get out of the car with her, and as she stood on the edge of the lock she described to him the swirling of the water as it poured from the Canal basin into the lock; the slow rising of the wide-beamed, coal-grimed little ship until it had been lifted from the level of Loch Fyne to that of the basin.

When the bridge swung back into position she drove over it on the last lap of the journey to Tarbert, and soon they were sweeping down a hill towards a natural, almost land-locked harbour where fishing boats nestled against a stone wharf and an old ruined castle on a hill towered above the squat shapes of wide-gabled houses. Turning right, they passed the dark tower of a church and drove to the other side of the isthmus of land to a pier where a sturdy ferry boat with a red and black funnel was preparing to set off for the distant islands.

Standing at last on the upper deck of the ferry boat, Deirdre watched the scene on the pier below. Seagulls, attracted by the activity, swooped about crying raucously: the air was damp, soft to the skin, and smelt of wet grass, pine trees and seaweed. The water of the sea loch was a smooth pewter grey, with here and there a patch of shimmering silver where pale sunlight was reflected.

The deck beneath their feet shuddered as engines throbbed and the ferryboat began to reverse away from the pier. Deirdre felt Rory tense beside her. Any sudden movement or noise seemed to put him on edge, she noticed, so now she explained quickly what was happening, thinking to reassure him. Throughout the car journey he had been very quiet, speaking only to answer her questions, and she found his withdrawn silences a little intimidating. Now she was aware of how many differences yawned between them, like ravines in a mountain range which might prove impossible to cross.

The ferryboat turned and headed for the open sea. Greyish green land scattered with wind-bent pines, edged by narrow sandy beaches and sharp upthrusting jagged rocks slid by. The sea-loch opened out, giving way to the sea, and the boat began to roll on the swell which set in from the distant ocean.

As the ferry chugged onwards the sky brightened in the west; a wide band of yellow light blinked from under the ragged edge of black cloud, and against the yellow she could see the curves of two mountains quite clearly. At once she told Rory about them.

'Those are two of the Bens, known as the Paps of Jura, and that's where we're going. There are really three mountains, but from this direction you'll only see two. None of them are very high—just over two thousand feet.'

'Have you climbed them?' she asked eagerly.

'I've *walked* up them, and it isn't easy. They're made of quartzite rock and as very little vegetation grows on that, so it breaks up into small sharp pieces. Walking on it is like walking on slippery gravel. For every step you take you slide back two. I was about fifteen when I first climbed them, and I spent the night on the top of the highest in a small tent.'

'Alone?'

'No, Jean and Douglas Fairlie were with me. We pretended we were climbing Everest, or at least I did.' The memory seemed to amuse him, and he laughed.

'I suppose you were staying on the island for your summer holidays?' she said, warmed by this little sidelight on his youth, and hoping to learn more.

'I suppose so,' he murmured, aggravatingly enigmatic. 'There's a legend about the mountains which you might like to know if you're keen on that sort of thing.'

'Please tell me.' She was unable to suppress a sigh of disappointment because he had not continued to talk about the times he had spent on the island. His hearing, made more acute by his inability to see properly, picked up the soft sound, and to her surprise he put an arm about her shoulders as if in a gesture of comfort.

'The two highest mountains are supposed to be the cairns raised over the graves of the two Danish outlaws who came to hide on the island. One was called Dim and one was called Rah. Their favourite occupation was robbery

46

with violence. You'll find the story in a book written by Doug Fairlie's grandfather, Alasdair Darroch—you may have heard of him.'

'Yes, I have. My mother used to talk about him, he was an authority on Celtic mythology.'

'That's right. And he wrote his books when he was living on the island, and Dougal and Jean used to visit him for their holidays. In fact we'll pass the house where he used to live on our way to the cottage—you won't miss it, it's a high dark building standing on cliffs overlooking a U-shaped bay. Are you impressed?'

'Oh, yes, I am! I'd no idea he had lived on the island,' she exclaimed delightedly. 'I wish. . . .'

She broke off, and stiffened involuntarily as she felt his fingers caress the back of her neck. His touch had the same peculiar effect she had experienced in his studio the night he had asked her to marry him; there was a possessiveness about it which she could not help but resent. So far he had made no attempt to make love to her and she had been glad, because she knew she was going to have difficulty in responding willingly and naturally. But she guessed he was a very physical person, more interested in action than in talking, and he would not be satisfied for long with a platonic friendship with the woman he had married.

Noticing that she had stiffened, Rory moved away from her, and at once tension sprang up between them.

'Do you own the cottage?' she asked hurriedly in an attempt to stop the tension from growing. 'Or do you just rent it?'

'It's mine. The old woman who used to live there left it to me in her will. She was some sort of relative of mine,' he replied indifferently. 'Have we far to go now?'

Questions swirled in her mind, wanting to be asked, but she suppressed them because she guessed he would either dodge them or not answer. He had made it very plain, from the beginning of their relationship, that anything he had done in the past was none of her business; all that mattered to him was the present. The past was over and the future could take care of itself, and he expected her to accept his outlook. But she found it difficult to do so because her own outlook was so very different—as far as she was concerned a person's past was as much a part of him as an arm or a leg, and she liked to know about it so that she could understand that person better. There was so much she did not understand about Rory.

'Not far,' she replied. 'I can see grey and white blobs which could be houses, and I can see some trees. Oh, and now I can see some small islands!'

'The Small Isles,' he said. 'We go between the most southerly of them and the mainland of Jura to reach the pier.'

As he spoke the ship's engines slowed down so that it could glide gently through the channel of water, and there was the pier with its angular white and red office buildings.

They disembarked without any trouble and were soon in the car again, driving towards the cluster of houses and the hotel at the head of the pier. On Rory's instructions Deirdre turned right, to follow a road which ran close to the coast past small cottages, each one set amongst cultivated fields behind dry-stone walls.

After a while there were no more houses, just brown curving moors lifting to the low grey cloud. The sea was hidden from view and the road wound onwards, seemingly to nowhere. Deirdre told Rory, and he suggested that she should start looking for a lane leading off to the right which would take them back to the coast.

The lane appeared and she turned on to it. The car bumped along the rough surface across more wet moorland, empty and lonely, above which a few seagulls hovered lazily. They were the only signs of movement.

Another road to nowhere, Deirdre was thinking, when it suddenly swooped downwards from the curving crest of the heather-brown moors in a series of bends; and there was the sea again, flat and grey, caught between two headlands making the U-shaped bay Rory had described. On one headland, looking remarkably forbidding on that still grey

48

day, stood a three-storeyed house of dark stone, set amongst a clump of wind-bent Scots pines.

'Oh!' gasped Deirdre, her lively imagination touched by the forbidding appearance of the house in that isolated place.

'What's the matter?' demanded Rory, feeling her shiver.

'The house is exactly as you described it. It's frightening.'

He laughed. 'I had a feeling it might make you shiver. It's supposed to be haunted.'

'It looks as if it should be. Who haunts it?'

'The ghost of a woman whose husband built the place. He pushed her off the cliff, so the story goes.' He sounded sceptical.

'Is it a true story?'

'As true, I suppose, as any story told by Alasdair Darroch. Myths are usually an exaggerated verion of what might have been true, aren't they? The ghost is supposed to appear when the moon is full. One night I stayed up and sat on the edge of the cliff where she was pushed over, but I didn't see her.'

'Ghosts have to be believed in to be seen. She probably didn't appear because she knew you were sceptical,' she teased.

'Probably,' he agreed with a grin.

The road climbed up to cross the headland close to the house. Deirdre had a brief glimpse of a man coming out of a side door, then she had to concentrate as the road twisted wickedly to the left and leapt down to another, smaller bay; a gently-curving bay rimmed with yellow sand, a bay which seemed to smile where the other one had scowled; an all-alone, secretive bay which seemed to be determined to guard its own tranquillity from invasion by the rest of the world. A small white cottage glinted beside the shore, its walls stark against the charcoal clouds. Behind it, up a hillside, stretched a patchwork of untilled fields overgrown with tussocky grass and blazing gorse bushes, and beyond it was a rocky ridge cutting it off from the next bay.

49

Delighted by what she saw, Deirdre stopped the car in front of the cottage where the road came to a convenient end.

'Are we there?' demanded Rory eagerly.

'Yes, we are. Oh, Rory, it's lovely. A perfect place for a. . . .' She broke off, suddenly embarrassed.

'For a honeymoon, you were going to say,' he said teasingly, as he fumbled for the door handle. 'You'll find the key above the door on a ledge; Mrs Buie who keeps an eye on the place when I'm not here said she'd leave it there.'

By the time she had found the key he was standing beside her. She managed to get the key into the lock but had difficulty in turning it, so he did so and the door swung back into a small porch where there was a cooker and shelves on which pans were arranged.

Deirdre was about to step into the porch when Rory placed a hand on her arm.

'Wait,' he said. 'I have to carry you.'

'Why?' she asked.

'I've been told it's the custom to carry the bride over the threshold,' he replied with a grin, 'and I'm not going to miss an opportunity like this!'

'I'm too heavy,' she demurred.

'I doubt it. Where are you?' he countered.

It seemed to her that he knew very well where she was, as he slipped one arm confidently about her shoulders and the other under her knees to lift her.

'Supposing you trip over the step,' she said faintly. Close to him for the first time, she was experiencing all sort of peculiar sensations.

'I won't. You forget I've been here before,' he replied, and stepped forward into the porch. 'There you are, nothing to it,' he added, allowing her to slip to the floor. Her heart beat wildly as she turned and opened the inner door which led from the porch into the house.

She stepped into a small dark hallway into which three doors opened, and choosing the one to the left she walked into a big room with a low ceiling. It had a window at either end and was furnished as a living kitchen, with a sink under one window and a table and chairs under the other. A peat fire smouldered in an old-fashioned fireplace, and in a deep alcove there was a double bed covered with a green candlewick bedcover. On the wall above the bed ticked an old wall clock in a handsome mahogany case.

'Oh, all the woodwork is painted pea-green,' gasped Deirdre. 'What a terrible colour!'

'There was probably a surplus of it at the general store,' Rory said. 'Mrs Buie told me the place needed some paint last year, so I told her to go ahead and do what she could. Is it clean?'

'Yes, and there's a fire in the hearth and the table is set for a meal. Why is there a bed in this room. Is it the only one?' she asked tentatively, and he smiled.

'No, there's a bedroom and a small bathroom, but we'll have to keep the fire going to get hot water. There's no immersion heater,' he replied.

He was feeling his way round the room slowly, making sure where each piece of furniture was positioned so that he could move about without guidance.

'Nothing seems to have changed since I was last here,' he murmured. 'As long as you don't move anything I'll be able to get about all right. I know the table is there by the window which faces the sea, and I can tell where windows are because the greyness isn't as dark.'

He sat down in an armchair and leaned back.

'I'm glad that journey is over,' he said, 'aren't you?'

'Yes. I'll bring in the food we've brought and make a meal.' Deirdre felt ridiculously cheerful. She had always liked playing house, and this cottage by the sea was to be their home for a few weeks. Here they would begin their life together, learn about each other—and possibly learn to love each other. The thought made her cheeks glow, and she hurried out into the damp cool air, forgetting momentarily that he could not see her blushing.

By the time they had eaten the meal the long northern

twilight was almost over, cut short that evening by the heavy rain clouds. In the darkening room flickering light from the peat fire gave the walls an orange glow which hid the nauseous green and struck glints of gold from brass ornaments, and found its reflection in the glass-fronted face of the old clock on the wall above the bed.

Deirdre had a sense of being in a different era of time; she felt cut off from everything she had ever known. The crackle of the fire and the ticking of the clock were the only sounds to be heard above the soft shushing of waves on the shore, and the tinkle of rain on the window pane. There was an atmosphere of sleepy intimacy in the room.

Aware suddenly that her head had nodded forward, Deirdre sat up, then sprang to her feet. The noise alerted Rory, who demanded to know where she was going.

'To fetch in the cases,' she replied, and fled outside again into the night and away from that intimacy.

She took Rory's case straight into the bedroom, which was furnished with a big double bed, chest of drawers, a wardrobe and a desk. She unpacked his clothing, hung some of it in the wardrobe and placed the rest in the drawers. Then she turned to the bed and lifted back the covers. It had been made with crisp white sheets which smelt of sun and wind, and warmed by an old-fashioned stone hot water bottle which was now cold. She took the bottle out.

Returning to the kitchen, she switched on the light. Rory had taken off his dark glasses and was rubbing his eyes, but as he heard her enter he stood up and took off his jacket, loosened his tie and slipped undone the top buttons of his shirt. In the glare of the electric light she could see that his face looked pale and drawn.

'Have you got a headache?' she asked. The journey must have been tiring for him as well as tedious and frustrating, because he had not been able to see places they had passed through and had to put up with someone else driving his car. She must remember that she was there to help ease his weariness, to make him comfortable. 'Shall I get you some aspirin?' she offered.

She started to move past him to empty the hot water bottle into the sink, but to her surprise he reached out a hand and caught her by the arm, swinging her round to face him. Clutching the hard bottle against her chest, she stared up at him. It seemed to her that his eyes, cloudy grey as the skies had been all day, stared back at her.

'No, I haven't a headache. Have you?' he asked softly. 'And what's this you're holding which is coming between us?'

'A stone hot water bottle—it was in the other bed. I've never seen one like it before, it must be antique. At least I know the bed in there is aired.' She was gabbling nervously, and he took the bottle from her and let it drop with a thud on the floor.

'I didn't marry just for you to drive me about, make my supper and get aspirin for me, you know,' he said teasingly, putting his arms round her and drawing her against him.

'I know,' she whispered, her cheek against his shoulder. She could feel the hardness of bone and the warmth of skin through the thin stuff of his shirt; then she felt his fingers at the nape of her neck. He pulled the pins out of her hair and it fell, heavy and silken and black as night, to cascade over her shoulders, down her back and forward over her breast.

Rory grasped a thick swathe of it in one of his hands.

'I've a vague memory of a fairy story about a girl who had very long hair,' he murmured, 'it was so long that she was able to twist it into a rope and let it down from the window of the tower where she was locked up. I believe her lover climbed up the rope of hair to the window.'

'That's the story of Rapunzel,' she whispered, 'but her hair was blonde in the picture in my story book.'

'Except for that, your hair is like hers, thick and strong enough to make a rope to climb up,' he said softly, framing her face with his hands.

She saw his mouth, the chiselled lips slightly parted, inches above hers. Then it was against hers, rough and urgent, compelling her to respond; and in that moment she

53

remembered Toni, and the way the sunlight shimmered on her blonde hair.

Deirdre awakened next morning to clear light coming through a window, and lay for a moment wondering where she was, surprised by the silence. No sound of traffic rumbling by, only the faint gurgling sound of water and the ticking of a clock.

She turned her head and looked at the clock and remembered where she was. She was in the bed in the kitchen in Rory's cottage, and she was alone.

Memories came, a flood of them rushing in, tumbling over each other. Memories of Rory kissing her, of her own inability to respond because his mention of blonde hair had brought the image of Toni vividly to her mind. Then she had recalled Dick Hunter's remark that Rory didn't love her, and the damage had been complete as she realised miserably that she was merely a substitute, and because Rory couldn't see her it was easy for him to pretend she was her Toni.

Revulsion of feeling had made her stiffen and twist her head to break the kiss. At first her attempted withdrawal had roused him, and for a few seconds she had felt the full force of his strength. He had tried to prevent her from breaking away and she had experienced a wild breathless feeling, a mixture of fear and desire, and she had realised that she would be helpless if he chose to exert his strength.

But instead he had released her, teasing her a little, saying that it was she who was tired and no wonder, after not having much sleep the night before on the train and then driving all that way. He had suggested politely—a little too politely for him—that she should sleep in the kitchen, and after saying goodnight he had gone to the bedroom and closed the door behind him.

Not wanting to dwell on those memories which had the power to make her feel guilty, Deirdre swung out of bed, dressed quickly in pants and shirt and washed her face at the sink in the soft water. Then she pinned up her hair, trying not to remember Rory's remarks about it, and went into the bedroom.

He was still asleep, his ruffled hair looking like dark flames against the white of the pillow. While she hovered in the doorway he moved, sighed deeply, muttered something and turned over. Cut to the quick by that subconscious murmur which had sounded suspiciously like the name Toni, Deirdre left the room hurriedly, and stepped outside.

The whole world was a-twinkle with light as rain-drenched moors reflected sunlight. In the bay the water seemed to beam benignly. A few birds, hopping about the branches of the two silver birches, twittered cheerfully and a nearby stream chuckled as it tumbled over its rocky bed towards the sea.

A feeling of joy leapt up within her because she was alive in such a lovely place, pushing out any other feeling. She went to the car to take out some of the boxes of photographic equipment for printing Rory's pictures of the expedition, and was just turning with a box to carry it into the cottage when a voice hailed her.

'Hello there! You're up early this morning.'

A man was coming from the direction of the stream. He was wearing waders which went up to his thighs, a tweed jacket over an open-necked shirt and a tweed hat the band of which was decorated with some colourful feathers which she realised were fishing flies. In one hand he carried a fishing rod and in the other some silvery fish. He was no taller than herself and under his dark eyebrows his eyes were dark brown. His mouth curved into a rather shy smile.

'I'm sorry if I startled you,' he said slowly, 'I've been fishing in the burn. I'm Dougal Fairlie from the big house yonder.'

He jerked his hea din the direction of the high headland where the tall house was a dark shape amongst its sheltering pines.

'I'm Deirdre Mallon,' she replied.

'Mallon?' he exclaimed, his black eyebrows going up in surprise.

'Yes, Rory and I arrived here yesterday afternoon.'

'Mrs Buie told us he was expected, but she said nothing about him bringing a wife. How long have you been married?'

'Since the day before yesterday,' she replied coolly.

Dougal stared. 'Well, now, this is a surprise. Is it true that his eyesight was affected by that climbing accident?'

'Yes, but the specialist says it will come back if Rory can relax and stop worrying about it. Its return is not only dependent on his health, but his attitude; that's why we've come here. We're going to work on a book of photographs of the expedition and . . .'

'Well, that's just fine,' he interrupted her quietly, and held out a hand to her. 'I'm pleased to meet you, Deirdre. Have you had your breakfast yet?'

'No, I came out to unpack some more equipment. This box is beginning to feel rather heavy—do you mind if I go in and put it down?'

'Ach, it's inconsiderate I am to keep you standing here! Let me help you.' He rested his fishing rod against the wall of the cottage and took the heavy box from her, carrying it with ease into the kitchen. 'I've some wee trout there you can have for your breakfast. You could be putting the kettle on to make a cup of tea while I bring in the rest of your stuff, and then I'll show you how to clean and cook the fish.'

He was as good as his word. Everything was brought in, then the fish were filleted with a few swift flashes of Dougal's sharp knife. In the storage cupboard which Mrs Buie had stocked with staple foods he found a bag of oatmeal, and coated the flesh of the fish with its pale brown crumbs. A lump of butter was melted in the frying pan on the stove and soon the fish were sizzling gently. By that time the kettle had boiled, and Deirdre made the tea and poured a cup for him.

Leaning against the table the dark, wide-shouldered, almost squat man sipped some of the tea and then gave her an odd underbrowed glance.

'Where did you meet Rory?' he asked abruptly.

'At a party.'

'Known him long?'

'No.' Deirdre flushed.

'Did you know him before the accident in which he lost his sight?'

'Not really. Why do you ask?'

A faint red ran up under his weatherbeaten skin.

'I expect you think I'm very rude asking such questions,' he muttered. 'It's just that I'm still surprised that Rory is married to you. Forgive me for saying so, but you're not the sort of woman I'd have expected to find in his company.'

His words brought Toni to mind again, slim, blonde, elegant and witty. Deirdre wasn't quite sure whether she should feel insulted or deflated by his remarks.

'I suppose you expected him to marry someone more sophisticated and better-looking,' she retorted, unable to keep her voice from shaking.

He noticed the shake and looked rather shame-faced.

'Now I've hurt your feelings, which is exactly what I wanted to avoid doing. Let me put it this way: in the first place I never expected Rory to marry, and in the second place I didn't realise he would ever have the good sense to choose someone like yourself to be his wife. There. Have I made amends?'

'Yes, you have.' She could not help smiling. 'He told me about you—he said he once climbed one of the mountains with you and your sister.'

Dougal shrugged. 'We were summer friends, once when he used to stay here with Miss Beaton. But that was some time ago, and a lot has happened to both of us since then. We no longer have much in common.' He pushed away from the table. 'I must go. My wee laddie Alan will be wondering where I am.'

'How old is he?'

'Five and a bit. We're staying here for the month with my mother.'

'Then I hope I'll meet him and your wife,' she said.

'My wife is dead.' The words seemed to be wrenched from him.

'I'm sorry.' Deirdre's easily-aroused compassion glowed in her eyes. Dougal noticed it, and his sallow-skinned, harsh-featured face softened slightly.

'Thank you,' he said. 'It happened five years ago. She was in an accident. I'll say good day to you now, and hope to see you again during your stay here.'

'You must come and see Rory,' she invited impulsively, 'he'll be glad to have a visitor.'

He gave her another odd glance but made no comment as he swung away through the door. She followed him, watched him take his fishing rod, and raised a hand in answer to his wave of farewell as he walked through the gate on to the road.

Going back to the kitchen she poured some tea for Rory and took the cup and saucer to the bedroom. He was still sprawled in the bed, his face half buried in the pillow.

'Rory, wake up!' she called cheerfully, going to stand by the bedside.

'I'm awake,' he growled without moving. 'Who were you talking to?'

'Dougal Fairlie. He'd been fishing in the burn, and he's given me some trout for your breakfast. They're cooking now, and I've brought you a cup of tea.'

He sat up, and pushed the hair back from his eyes. He was frowning and looked thoroughly disgruntled.

'It's a lovely day,' she said brightly, 'you should see the view from the window.'

'I wish I could,' he countered acidly, and she gasped as if he had hit her.

'I'm sorry,' she muttered, 'I forgot. You didn't seem blind. . . .' She had been going to say 'last night', then thought better of it, but he had noticed her slip, and his mouth curved sardonically as he finished the sentence for her.

'Last night. That's what you were going to say, isn't it? Well, some things are instinctive and a man doesn't need his sight to do them. Where's the tea?'

Still quivering from that sharp rejoinder, she held out the cup and saucer, without thinking to take his hand and guide it. His groping fingers knocked the cup flying and hot liquid spilt on him, making him yelp with surprise, then swear.

Appalled, Deirdre went down on her knees beside the bed to pick up the fallen cup. When she had it she stood up again and placed it on the saucer.

'I'm sorry, Rory,' she murmured. He was leaning back against the brass railings of the bedhead and his eyes were closed. Tears welled in her eyes; thinking to do good she had tried too hard, and had earned his contempt.

'Stop saying you're sorry about everything,' he said quietly, 'you can't help it if I knock a cup over. It wasn't your fault. Now go away while I get up and get dressed—at least that's something I can do without your help.'

In the kitchen Deirdre set the table, cut bread and buttered it, and all the time she thought about Rory. His brittle mood must be due to him having woken hopefully, only to find he still couldn't see. He must waken like that every morning, she thought, and the tears ran down her face.

He came into the room and walked straight to the table as if he could see, found his chair and sat down. Deirdre went out to the kitchen to bring in the fish. She put his plate in front of him and then poured more tea and sat down.

'The cup and saucer are on your right,' she said in a small miserable voice.

'Thanks.'

'Rory, I'm . . .'

'If you're going to say you're sorry again I'll have to spank you,' he cut in with his quick grin. 'Don't be sorry—if you're going to pity me all the time and think of me as an invalid who has to be waited on, we'll not have any fun this summer. Now stop snivelling.'

'I'm not snivelling,' she retorted, annoyed that he had noticed.

'Yes, you are. You've been crying because I bawled at you in the bedroom, haven't you?'

'How do you know?'

'I could hear you. Blindness seems to have improved my hearing. It's also increased my selffishness and has possibly exaggerated all my other faults, so you'll have to watch out for yourself, love.'

'But I wasn't crying because you shouted at me,' she explained slowly, wanting to have everything straight between them, 'I was upset because I feel so inadequate. I try hard to help you and I end up by doing everything wrong. Rory, about last night, I'm afraid I wasn't—I couldn't . . .'

'Forget it. I have,' he said gruffiy. 'And here's a piece of good advice; never rake over dead ashes. It doesn't do any good. We'll get used to each other after a while.'

She didn't persist and there was silence while they both finished their breakfast.

'The fish tasted good,' observed Rory eventually. 'I wonder if I could fish—perhaps I could if you were with me. You'd have to attach the flies or put the bait on the hook, and tell me when I had a bite. Have you ever done any fishing?'

'No, I'm afraid I haven't,' she admitted, wishing that she had. She wondered if anyone would teach her how so that she could help him.

'Dougal's a good fisherman and has lots of patience,' he commented. 'I bet he was surprised when you told him you and I are married.'

'Yes, he was—he said he didn't think you'd have had enough sense to marry someone like me,' she said with a laugh.

'Oh, he did, did he? I'm glad you think that's funny.'

'It's sad that his wife was killed in an accident, isn't it?' she said.

Rory didn't reply immediately, so she looked up at him. He had gone very pale.

'What accident?' he asked at last, his voice huskier than usual. 'When did it happen?'

'I don't know what sort of accident. Dougal seemed to find it difficult to talk about, so I didn't press him. It happened five years ago.'

She stopped as she saw him stiffen. Now his face was paper white and he'd closed his eyes.

'Rory, are you all right? You look as if you've had a shock. Did you know her?'

'Yes, I knew her,' he muttered. He rubbed his fingers against his eyes and then opened them. 'As soon as you've finished clearing away we'll make a plan of campaign for working on the book,' he said in a brisk, autocratic voice. 'I suggest we work every morning on the writing. I kept a diary of all that happened and made a note of each photograph I took. Selecting the photographs is going to take time. The film is developed and I've brought the negatives. You'll have to make the prints, and describe each one to me so that I can identify it; and unless my sight comes back pretty soon you'll have to decide which are the best of them.'

It was quite obvious that the death of Dougal's wife, which was such a shock to him, was not to be discussed any more. Deirdre was beginning to suspect that he pushed anything which hurt his feelings into some deep recess of his mind, in an attempt to forget it. He didn't like to admit to sentiment, or to being hurt by people or events, and she could not help wondering what had happened to him when he was younger to make him like that.

'You'd really trust me to choose the photographs?' she asked.

'I'll have to,' he replied with a touch of dryness. 'One of the reasons why I thought you'd be such a help is that you see things in the same way I do—I can tell that by the way you describe everything. While I can't see you can be my eyes.'

She was a little overwhelmed by this. Such trust from him was alarming, and had the effect of putting her on her mettle. She had to do her best for him.

'This book isn't the official written description of the

expedition,' Rory went on, 'Dick will be doing that. This is my impression of what happened, using the camera as the medium. So the writing will be brief and confined to naming places and people in the photographs, with perhaps an anecdote or two when applicable.'

'It isn't going to be easy being your eyes in that way,' she murmured. 'I might select the wrong photographs.'

'I know it isn't going to be easy, and I know I'll get very frustrated because I can't see the photos. Do you think you'll be able to put up with me? I don't want you snivelling every time I yell at you. I'd prefer it if you'd yell back at me,' he said with a grin.

Deirdre chuckled as she tried to imagine herself yelling at him.

'What's funny?' he demanded.

'The idea of me yelling at you. I've never yelled at anyone in my life. I wouldn't know how.'

'Stay with me for a while and you'll soon learn,' he retorted. Then the amusement faded from his face, and he frowned and rubbed his forehead with his fingers. 'Gently-reared, a sensitive plant. That's what Dick said about you,' he mused. 'Then he had the nerve to ask me if I knew what I was doing when I asked you to marry me.'

'He told me he wondered if you knew,' she said quietly.

'You know what he was getting at, don't you?' he asked roughly.

'I decided that he was concerned about you because you were marrying a woman you'd never seen,' she replied shakily.

'But I have seen you. I saw you at that party.'

'And you didn't remember me,' she reminded him.

'I did when you described yourself,' he argued stubbornly.

'Are you sure? Are you sure you didn't create someone in your imagination to fit the description I gave you?' she challenged.

He was silent and she guessed she had hit on the truth, but the knowledge gave her no comfort.

'You're wrong about Dick, though,' he said abruptly, 'he wasn't concerned about me, he knows me too well. He was worried about someone like you marrying someone like me.'

'But why should he be worried?'

He sighed and thrust a hand through his hair so that it stood up like a cock's comb.

'Oh, hell, I don't know,' he growled. 'He said there could be too many differences between us. He said he could see you're an intelligent, sensitive woman who's been well educated, and that you were probably brought up in a good home. He said you must be out of your mind to agree to marry an egotistical ruffian like me.'

Out of your mind. Elise had made the same comment. If she heard it applied to herself many more times she would begin to believe it, thought Deirdre ruefully.

'And I suppose you told him that your marriage to me was none of his business,' she said calmly.

'I did, in much more colourful language than you'd ever use,' he admitted with a grin. 'Well, it's going to be interesting this summer finding out whether I did know what I was doing—even if I couldn't see what I was doing when I asked you to marry me, and if you were sane when you agreed—isn't it?'

'Yes, I suppose it is,' she replied rather faintly.

'And now I'd like to get down to some work. I thought we'd use the bedroom as a study. There's a desk in there and we can always leave the stuff lying around and close the door on it if we want to go out or if anyone visits us. You can sit at the desk and type and I'll lie on the bed and dictate to you.'

'Lazy thing,' she taunted lightly, beginning to collect the empty dishes together.

Rory stood up and she heard him move behind her. Too late she guessed what he was going to do in retaliation to her taunt. As her hands went up to the nape of her neck he grasped them easily in one of his, and with the other pulled her hair so that it came spilling down over her shoulders. She heard him laughing as he moved away towards the door, and she knew with that strange new feeling compounded of fear and excitement that while she lived with him here, in this isolated place, she was completely at the mercy of his superior physical strength and unpredictable temperament.

CHAPTER FOUR

THE grey car bumped over the uneven surface of the road, splashed through some puddles and slowed down to take a bend. The weather was wet and windy; trees and bushes tossed their branches. Dark clouds raced across the sky and flurries of rain sluiced down the windscreen in grey curtains of water, making it difficult for Deirdre to see where she was going in spite of the hardworking wipers.

The stormy day had come as a surprise after a week of fine weather; a week of high pale skies and yellow sunshine, pearl-misted mornings, golden afternoons, flaming sunsets and long blue-shadowed twilights. During that week Deirdre had come to terms with the domestic arrangements of the cottage, and had learned how to work with Rory.

She bit her lip and her hands clenched on the steering wheel. She had not as yet learned to live with him in the fullest sense, and as a result, the silent nerve-cracking tension growing between them had driven her from the cottage today, using the excuse that they needed to replenish their stocks of food to escape for a few hours.

A movement on the road ahead caught her attention. Someone was walking along, and as she drew nearer she recognised the wide swinging shoulders under the Harris tweed jacket, the old fly-decorated hat and the high waders. Stopping beside him, she rolled down the window and called,

'Would you like a lift?'

'Well now,' said Dougal Fairlie, slowly turning to look at her, 'that's kind of you. It's a good day for the fish but not for mere men, and all I can think of is getting back home to sit before a fire with a cup of hot tea and some of my mother's buttered scones to eat. I'll accept the lift if you'll agree to come in when we get to the house, and have a cup of tea with us.'

'I'd like that,' she replied, ignoring the voice of conscience which accused her of looking for a way to avoid being alone with Rory.

Dougal placed his fishing basket and rod in the back seat and climbed in beside her, bringing with him a smell of damp tweed and pipe tobacco.

'We've been expecting you or your mother to call on us,' said Deirdre as the car eased forward.

'Well now, have you?' he said. She waited for him to say more, but he didn't, and she realised that there was a reserve in his manner which she had not noticed at their first meeting.

'Why haven't you come?' she persisted.

'Ach, we've been a wee bit hesitant because we weren't sure we'd be welcome,' he replied.

'Oh! Why should you feel like that?' she exclaimed.

'Have you forgotten that you and Rory are on your honeymoon? That's no time to be having your neighbours dropping in on you to pass the time of day,' he said so smoothly that she had a suspicion it wasn't the only reason for him not having called.

Colour washed up over her face. She could hardly tell him that she and Rory were not honeymooners in the accepted sense, that you had to be in love to have a honeymoon and Rory was not in love with her. As for herself ... again she bit her lip. What were her feelings about Rory? Compassion, because such a vigorous person could not see. Admiration for his courage and determination. And above all fear, this terrible irrational fear which made her pull away from him every time he touched her, which had made it impossible for her to let him make love to her.

'It's nice of you to be so considerate,' she said quickly, realising that her wandering thoughts had produced a noticeable silence, 'but Rory is beginning to think you haven't called on us because he's offended your family in some way. Has he?'

She felt Dougal shift in his seat, and glancing sideways saw that he had brought out his pipe. He put it between his lips but made no effort to light it as he stared straight ahead with narrowed eyes. Quiet, slow of speech and movement, he was in direct contrast to Rory, whose lively mind and ruthlessness expressed itself all the time in quick decisive movement and rough, often staccato speech.

'It's hard to say,' he murmured eventually. 'He may have done. On the other hand, he may not have done.'

'Well, really,' she exclaimed with a little laugh, 'what a strange answer! Surely you must know whether he has or not!'

'I know it sounds strange, but that's how it is. I can't be one hundred per cent sure that he did what he's supposed to have done; all I know is that he was capable of doing it.'

'Are you going to tell me what it is he's supposed to have done?' she queried, a little irritated with his slow non-committal answers.

'I can't. You'll have to find out from someone else. You see, it isn't the sort of thing I could tell a young bride about her husband while they're on their honeymoon.'

His answer chilled her blood and dried her throat. She swallowed nervously as she turned the car on to the moor road. Questions popped into her mind, longing to be asked.

'Oh, dear,' she sighed. 'Now you've made him sound like a criminal of some sort—I hope he didn't take anything from you and not return it. Boys have a way of borrowing books or equipment and forgetting to return them to their owners, but it's usually sheer forgetfulness, although at the time it might look like stealing.'

He stiffened, and again she gave him a quick glance. Some of the colour had receded from his weather-beaten face. His firm rather small mouth under the long beaky nose quirked sensitively.

'What you have just said could be exactly what happened,' he said, 'but why do you say *boys*?'

'Because Rory was only fifteen when he last visited the island,' she said.

'That isn't so. He was here five years ago.'

Deirdre absorbed that piece of information while she guided the car carefully over a particularly rough piece of road. Rory's refusal—or was it just an inability to talk about himself?—to tell her about anything he had done in the past could make her appear strangely ignorant about her own husband. She could think of nothing to say, and was glad when Dougal made an effort to change the subject, almost as if he had sensed he had upset her.

'And how are you getting along with the preparation of the book?' he asked.

'Quite well. We work every morning on it, and sometimes in the evenings too. Rory kept a diary of all events, and I read what he wrote, then he helps me to compose a narrative to accompany the photographs.'

'That sounds interesting,' Dougal observed.

'Oh, it is! After working on it some mornings I'm quite surprised when I look out of the window and see the heather in bloom on the moors and realise I'm on an island in the Hebrides and not amongst the Mountains of Kumoa in the Himalayas.'

'And how are you liking our island?'

'Very much, although I haven't seen much. We go for walks in the afternoon along the beach.'

'I haven't seen you coming towards the headland.'

'No, usually we go the other way—Rory likes to sit on the rocks where the burn falls into the sea. He likes the sound of the water tumbling over the rocks. It's a beautiful place and there are all kinds of birds to watch.'

'You must see more,' he told her. 'We shall have to arrange to take you to other parts. There are standing stones on the other side of the island, and raised beaches,

67

and some interesting caves at Corpach where, it's said, the boats carrying the dead on their way to be buried on the island of Oronsay used to take shelter. There are no roads going there, so it's necessary to walk over the moors, and sometimes on the way one comes across a herd of deer.'

Deirdre sighed. 'I would like to see more, only Rory couldn't walk over rough ground and he wouldn't be able to see anything.'

'He's seen it all before,' Dougal said. 'But surely he wouldn't object if you left him for a short while to see something for yourself? After all, you might never come here again.'

'That's true. I might never come here again,' she repeated in a rather forlorn voice.

The deep U-shaped bay of grey wind-tossed water had come into view, and on its headland the tall dark house glowered menacingly. Within a few minutes Deirdre stopped the car in front of the house, and Dougal opened the door on his side and leaned into the back to take his fishing equipment.

'Come away now into the house,' he said as he got out of the car.

They hurried through the wild skin-stinging raindrops round to the side entrance of the house and into a porch. Dougal removed his waders, damp jacket and hat, then he helped Deirdre to take off her anorak and led her through an inner door into a big warm kitchen.

A small, sturdily built woman with grey-sprinkled dark hair wound round her head in a braid was just placing a kettle on a ring on the stove. She looked round as they entered and smiled, her dark deep-set eyes shining with a friendly light.

'I saw you arrive, and I was hoping Dougal would bring you in.' She came forward and held out a hand to Deirdre. 'You're Rory's wife, aren't? I'm Margot Fairlie.'

'I'm pleased to meet you, Mrs Fairlie, and I'm so excited to be in the house where Alasdair Darroch wrote his wonderful books. My mother was very interested in Celtic mythology, and had read all of them.'

'And I'm thinking that is why she called you Deirdre,' said Margot with a smile. 'That story was one of my own favourites, but I hope you're going to be luckier than Deirdre of the Sorrows, for although she had the richest and the best of life during her short stay in Scotland with Naisi, she had to pay for it with her life when she returned to Ireland. When you've had your tea I'll take you to see my father's study and show you his desk and some of his manuscripts if you like.'

'Yes, I would,' replied Deirdre, feeling at ease at once with this gentle understanding woman.

'Then come to the sitting room. Wee Alan is there with Kirsty. She's playing snakes and ladders with him, Dougal. She's very patient with him. I don't know where the twins are.'

'They're probably in the attic,' replied Dougal, 'it's always been a good place to play on a wet day.'

Margot's eyes crinkled at the corners as she smiled again at Deirdre.

'Even your husband has played up there on a wet day in the summer, Deirdre,' she said. 'It seems a long time ago now.'

'I'm going upstairs to find some shoes,' said Dougal, moving to the door. 'I'll tell the twins to come down, shall I?'

'Yes, please. Tell them I've just taken some drop scones from the griddle, that should tempt them,' said Margot.

She took Deirdre along a passage into a wide light room. Lace curtains were looped back from a bay window which faced the sea. Heavy Victorian furniture, dark and glossy, seemed to fill every corner of the room and huge sepia engravings of Highland scenery hung on the walls.

Before the fire two people were sitting on the floor facing each other across a low table on which a game was set out; one of them was a small boy with a mop of mouse-coloured hair clustering about his thin elfin face, who turned to look at Deirdre with glistening grey eyes, strangely empty of expression. The other person was a slim woman of about thirty years of age, whose brown hair had a chestnut sheen and whose eyes shimmered with brilliant blue light when she also turned to look at Deirdre.

'Kirsty, Alan, I'd like you to meet Deirdre Mallon,' said Margot. 'She's going to have a cup of tea with us. Now you talk to her while I go and finish setting the tea trolley. That's a fine wee game you've been having, Alan.'

'Where's Daddy?' the boy asked. 'I want to see him. Did he catch any fish?'

'He's upstairs just now. You stay here. . . .'

'I don't want to.' The boy was petulant. 'I'm going to see Daddy. I'm tired of playing games with her!' Springing to his feet, the boy pointed at Kirsty, and whirling round he ran from the room. They could hear his feet pattering on the stairs and his voice calling shrilly to his father.

Margot Fairlie looked vaguely troubled and apologetic.

'I'm sorry, Kirsty, that he should speak to you like that when you've been so patient with him.'

'That's all right, Mrs Fairlie,' replied Kirsty with a sweet smile. Her voice was clear and cool. 'It will take time for him to get used to me, and I have plenty of time.'

'Please sit down, Deirdre, and make yourself comfortable. Kirsty is . . . was . . . an old friend of my daughter-in-law's, and has just come back to Scotland from Canada where she has been working for the last four years.' Margot hesitated, then hurried from the room, saying something about having to take more scones from the oven.

Deirdre sat down slowly on the edge of a big couch covered with faded red plush. She was suddenly very conscious of her appearance as she noticed the blue eyes flicking over her critically.

She wished she wasn't wearing her old blue jeans and rather faded tight-fitting red shirt, she wished she had thought to look in the mirror in the porch to make sure her hair was tidy. She wished she was wearing some make-up.

The neatness of Kirsty's knife-pleated grey skirt and pretty blouse, the smoothness of her thick short hair and the

70

slimness of her figure, made Deirdre feel not only untidy but overgrown and fat! Literally fat, even though she knew that she was really only big-boned, square-shouldered and full-breasted.

'So you're Rory's wife,' drawled Kirsty, rising lithely to her feet and sitting down in the armchair behind her. 'Well, well! You're not really the sort of person I'd have expected Rory, with his passion for beauty and elegance, to choose. How is he?'

Swallowing what amounted to a downright insult, Deirdre tried to answer coolly,

'Very well. Do you know him?'

'Yes, I do. I met him five years ago. I went to school with Sorcha Fairlie, and she and I were always good friends. She invited me here for a holiday that year, and Rory was at his cottage. We saw a lot of him. You know about Sorcha, I suppose?'

'It's an unusual name.'

'It's Gaelic for Clare, and means *light*. She was like a light—dainty, fair-haired, luminous skin, glistening grey eyes. She seemed to twinkle, and like a light she went out suddenly.' Kirsty snapped her fingers, 'just like that.'

'She was Dougal's wife?' guessed Deirdre. 'He told me she was killed in an accident.'

Kirsty raised her finely-plucked arched eyebrows in surprise.

'Dougal told you?' she queried. 'Not Rory?'

'No, he's never mentioned her. He . . . he doesn't talk much about the past . . . his past, I mean,' replied Deirdre defensively, as she noticed the blue eyes narrow and the thin firm mouth curve sardonically. 'I don't think he knew she was dead until I told him what Dougal had said. He was a little shocked, but then I expect you all were. What happened?'

'She'd gone to Glasgow—she left here without a word to anyone. Dougal wasn't here. He was attending a conference somewhere. He's an assistant professor at a university,' said Kirsty. 'Rory had left the island the day before to return to

London. Sorcha had followed him and was killed by a car when she stepped off the curb without looking to cross Argyle Street.'

'Followed him?' Deirdre was puzzled. 'Why should she follow Rory?'

Kirsty's smile had a strangely pitying quality. As she heard the squeak of the wheels of a tea trolley being pushed along the passage towards the sitting room, her eyes flashed a warning and she put a pointed finger against her lips. Then she said,

'Your guess is as good as mine or anyone else's. What did you do for a living before you married Rory?'

'I still do it, or shall when term begins,' Deirdre realised from the swift change of subject that the matter of Sorcha's death was not to be discussed in front of Margot Fairlie. 'I teach.'

'Primary or infants?' Again the critical blue glance swept over her.

'Secondary. I have a degree in history.'

'Like Dougal. I think you'd have a lot in common with him—much more than you have with that fascinating husband of yours,' drawled Kirsty. 'Has Rory ever seen you?'

'Once. Last year at a party,' replied Deirdre coldly. She was beginning to feel needled by the other woman's patronising manner.

'Really? I didn't realise you'd known him that long.'

'We didn't meet again until he was hurt and in hospital. I visited him.'

'Aha! So that's how it was done—you played the part of the ministering angel. Not the first time a man has fallen for that line, particularly a blind man who needs all the help he can get.' Kirsty smiled provocatively, then with a complete change of manner as Margot appeared in the doorway with a tea trolley, she sprang to her feet and went forward saying, 'Here, let me help you with that.'

'Thank you, Kirsty. We'll put it beside the couch and I'll sit beside Deirdre; I only wish Rory were here with us,' said Margot.

'He would like you to come and see him,' said Deirdre. She found Margot's warm kindliness a welcome relief after the cold cut and thrust of the conversation with Kirsty. It was like having a mother again. 'He's still diffident about going out, especially to someone else's house.'

Margot nodded understandingly as she poured tea into a cup.

'I know, he's afraid he'll walk into something or knock something over. It was a terrible thing to happen to him, blindness, however temporary it might be, is very limiting for anyone, but even more for someone like Rory, so full of life. Everything that ever mattered to him—climbing, camping, sailing——'

'Beautiful women,' put in Kirsty under her breath, but Deirdre heard her and gave her a sharp glance.

'—Fishing, his work as a photographer.' Either Margot hadn't heard the whispered comment, or she was deliberately ignoring it, 'all are lost to him unless some effort can be made by the rest of us to help him to have some of them. I believe you're helping him to get a book ready about the expedition? He's fortunate that you're capable of helping him with it.'

'I should have thought any little typist could have helped him with that,' mocked Kirsty.

'No, I can't agree,' contradicted Margot gently. 'It has to be someone who is able to see as he sees. Don't forget he isn't able to select the photographs himself.'

'Oh, I wish you'd come and see him!' exclaimed Deirdre impulsively. She felt that the older woman's understanding of Rory would help him to bear his affliction more easily.

'I'd have come before this and I know the twins have been longing to call on you, but when Dougal told us you were only just married I thought it would be best to wait a while. A honeymoon is meant to be spent in privacy and peace.'

Encountering Kirsty's bright mocking glance again, Deirdre felt herself blush. It was as if the other woman had guessed that there was no real honeymoon and was amused by the situation.

The arrival in the room of two children created a welcome diversion. About twelve years of age, they were tall and gangling with narrow sallow faces, dark eyes brimming with mischief and short black hair and, since they were both dressed in long tartan pants and blue cotton sweaters, it was difficult to tell whether they were boys or girls. They seemed to swoop down on the tea trolley to grab buttered drop scones, then flung themselves down on the floor and stared with interest at Deirdre.

'Who's she?' demanded one of them, the one who was the thinner and more angular of the two and who could be a boy.

'Geordie, your manners are a disgrace to the Fairlies family,' Margot rebuked him gently. 'This is Deirdre. She's married to Rory.'

'Can we visit him?' demanded the other dark-eyed child. 'We want to ask him what it was like when he fell down that mountain.'

'Please excuse them, Deirdre,' said Margot. 'These two are Beth—she's the nearest one—and Geordie Whyte, my daughter's twin scamps. She and her husband Murray are away sailing in their motor-cruiser among the Outer Hebrides. Usually these two go with them, but this year Jean and Murray felt a need for a holiday by themselves.' Margot tried to look severe, but failed as she glanced at the twins. 'I can't say I blame your parents for wanting to be without you two for a while, either,' she added, and they both grinned.

'Can we visit Rory?' persisted Beth. 'I remember him. Even though we were only seven when he came here last, he took us on all sorts of adventures.'

'Don't let them bother him, Deirdre,' said Margot anxiously, 'not if you think he isn't up to it yet.'

'I think he'd be glad if they came over to see him,' said Deirdre.

'Me too?' asked a treble voice from the doorway. Alan

had come back, and was riding piggyback on his father's shoulders.

'You too,' Deirdre smiled at him, and felt inordinately pleased when he smiled shyly back at her. She guessed that he did not smile readily at strangers.

'And me?' Kirsty asked in imitation of the boy. 'Or are visiting times restricted to children and grandmothers?'

'And you, and Dougal,' replied Deirdre steadily. Kirsty had a way of speaking which made her feel uncomfortable; there was a bitterness in the woman's attitude which did not match her beauty. She was like canker-eaten fruit, sound and smooth on the outside, soured and rotten within.

'It might be a wee bit overwhelming for Rory if we all turn up,' said Dougal in his slow way, as he lowered Alan into an armchair and then sat down in front of him on the edge of the seat.

'But if we're all there when you meet him, you'll find it far easier to break the ice,' said Kirsty, and he turned to give her a slow considering glance from under his beetling black eyebrows.

'And what makes you think there's any ice to break?' he countered.

Kirsty shrugged her slim shoulders.

'You've made no effort to go and see him, so I assumed that you're still holding him responsible for what happened to Sorcha five years ago,' she said calmly, returning his gaze steadily.

Dougal brought out his pipe and began to stuff tobacco into the bowl, apparently finding the whole process very absorbing. After a sharp glance in his direction Margot made a lot of unnecessary noise lifting the teapot lid to glance in it, then she sent one of the twins for hot water and began to ask Deirdre questions about her family and her work, obviously working hard to cover up an awkward moment.

The awkwardness passed, conversation became more general and soon Deirdre was following Margot up a curving staircase to the second floor of the house on her way to the study where Alasdair Darroch had written his books.

It was a small neat room at the front of the house, and its window had extensive views of the bay and the sea beyond.

'On a good day it's possible to see right down as far as Gigha and even to the Mull of Kintyre,' said Margot. 'My father used to say that if the visibility was very good he could see Rathlin Island off the north coast of Ireland—with binoculars, of course.'

'Jura is an ideal place for writing, I should think,' said Deirdre. 'It's so quiet and isolated and stimulating to the imagination. Do you live here all the time?'

'No, and we never have. We only come for the summer. Sometimes Ian, my husband and I come in May for a week, to open up the house and air everything after the winter, and he and I often like to have a holiday here in early October. He's had to go to Glasgow for a business meeting, but he'll be back again next week.'

'Will your daughter be coming here to collect the twins when she returns from her cruise?'

'Aye, Jean will be coming here. Nothing will keep her away! She loves the island, as we all do. Its name means "Island of Deer", because of the many herds of deer which roam across it, but Jean always calls it her "dear" island.'

'Rory told me about the time he took her and Dougal climbing with him,' Deirdre said.

Margot smiled reminiscently.

'I remember. He took them up Beinn an Oir, the highest one—its name means Hill of Gold. But they also climbed the other two, Beinn Siantadh—the Hallowed Mountain—and Beinn a Chaolais—the Mountain of the Strait. Ach, he had us worried, Miss Beaton and I! We thought they'd gone for an afternoon tramp only. When they didn't return I had all sorts of visions of them having fallen and hurt themselves and she was worried, poor old soul, because he was only allowed to come here for his holidays if she paid his fare and made sure he didn't get into any mischief. The last was almost impossible, because he was much too strong-willed for her even at fifteen years of age.'

'He told me she was some sort of relative of his,' Deirdre remarked.

'Yes, that's so. She was his great-aunt. He's the son of her only niece, the daughter of her brother, Roderick Beaton, from whom Rory get his first name. I can see you're looking a wee bit puzzled.'

'Yes, I am. You see, Rory has told me nothing about his family—he says there's nothing to tell. He doesn't seem to realise that knowing more about him might help me to understand him a little better.'

'Then I shall tell you all I know, all that Miss Beaton told me—and that wasn't much, because she was a close-mouthed, proud old lady,' said Margot kindly. 'Rory was orphaned when he was a baby, and at first he was looked after by his grandmother, his mother's mother. Then she was taken ill and he was put into a foster home.'

'Oh.' Deirdre was a little taken aback. 'Couldn't Miss Beaton have given him a home?'

'If she'd known where to find him I think she might have done, although it wouldn't have been easy because she was a single woman and the matron of a hospital.'

'Why couldn't she find him?'

'Ach, it's one of those complicated stories about the break-up of a family, the sort of thing that happens when roots are pulled up and members of a family lose touch with each other. Grace and Roderick Beaton were born in that cottage where you're living, and where Beatons had lived for generations; but like many other young people of their generation they left the island for the mainland, thinking to better themselves.'

'Where did they go? What did they do?'

Margot sighed. 'He went into the Merchant Navy, as many men from the Hebridean Islands have always done, and she went into nursing. He married a girl in his home port and they had a daughter. Then Roderick contracted a disease when he was at sea and died abroad somewhere. His wife married again and didn't keep in touch with Grace Beaton, and the link was broken. Years later Grace came

77

across a probationer in a hospital where she was a ward Sister who turned out to be her niece. The girl hadn't been happy with her stepfather, and was glad to find her father's only relative alive. The war came, and Grace was made a Matron of an Army hospital, but she kept in touch with her niece through writing. She heard all about the handsome fighter pilot the girl had met and fallen in love with.'

'He was Rory's father?' guessed Deirdre.

Margot nodded.

'Yes, it was one of those brief wartime affairs. They married on one of his leaves, then he went off and was killed in a dogfight over the Channel. The girl discovered she was pregnant; he hadn't told her where his parents lived so she couldn't contact them, so she went home to her mother and the baby was born. She must have died soon afterwards, because Grace didn't hear from her again.'

'How sad,' murmured Deirdre, and Margot shrugged.

'Yes, it was, yet not unusual for that period of time. When the war was over Miss Beaton made an attempt to trace her sister-in-law and find Rory, but by the time she had caught up with him his grandmother was already dead and he was in a foster home. Miss Beaton herself was ready to retire and come to live here, and she managed to persuade the welfare authorities to let Rory come and stay with her for the summer holidays, which he did for three years on the run.' Margot smiled reminiscently. 'I'll not forget the day Jean brought a tall, skinny, rough-haired boy home with her. She'd met him on the moors. Well, have I filled in a few missing details for you? I'm afraid I know nothing more.'

'Yes, you have. I understand much better now.'

'And that's all to the good, I'm sure. I expect Rory has inherited a little of the Beaton pride and reserve; he probably doesn't think it's necessary to explain himself, or doesn't understand that it's sometimes important to ask a few questions and give a few answers, so as to avoid being misunderstood.'

Margot's face clouded a little, and Deirdre guessed that

she was thinking of the suggestion Kirsty had made about Rory being indirectly responsible for Sorcha's death. She waited hopefully, but in the next instant Margot smiled, squeezed her arm and added sincerely,

'I'm so glad he found someone like you, Deirdre, just when he needed you most.'

Deirdre flushed. 'It's kind of you to say so—I do my best to help him, but sometimes it's difficult. He gets very frustrated. I wish you'd visit us, he thinks he's done something to offend you, and that's why you haven't been.'

Again Margot looked troubled.

'It would be easier if Jean were here,' she said, 'she was always his friend, they're the same age and have the same adventurous spirit. Dougal is a few years younger and a bit puritanical in outlook, I say it even though I'm his mother,' Margot added with a chuckle. 'He would never have stayed out all night on Beinn and Oir if he hadn't been too afraid to try and find his way back alone. And I think there have been times when he's been a little shocked by Rory's way of life over the past few years. But you and I could talk for hours, and I think I should tell you it's gone six o'clock, and Rory might be wondering where you are.'

Deirdre's conscience worked overtime as she drove to the cottage as fast as she dared. The little house looked as serene as ever, even in the wild violet light of the stormy day, and the small bay was so sheltered that only a few white crests of waves disturbed the purple-grey of its surface.

The brakes screeched as she stopped the car, and in a few seconds she was out of it, her arms full of grocery bags. She burst into the porch, her heart pounding, suddenly afraid of what she might find. Supposing Rory, frustrated by his inability to see properly and made furious by her absence, had done something desperate?

Urging herself to calm down, she tiptoed through the kitchen door and stood just inside the room. It was dim, because of the heavy clouds outside. The fire flickered in the grate and the sound of music came softly from the transistor radio. Everything seemed quiet and peaceful.

Rory was sitting at the table and in his hands he held a single lens reflex camera, the sort used by professional photographers. Another camera was on the table, with some cardboard boxes which held rolls of unexposed film. Holding her breath, Deirdre watched him insert a roll of film into the camera and snap it shut.

A thought came winging wildly through her mind: *he could see?* The next moment her heart seemed to leap into her throat as he turned his head, and appeared to look straight at her. Tensely, she waited for him to speak.

CHAPTER FIVE

THE silence which stretched between them was taut, like a wire stretched to breaking point. Deirdre felt her muscles aching with the effort to keep still. She wanted to speak, to ask Rory if he could see, but the words would not form themselves because she realised with a quiver of guilt that she did not want to know and, what was worse, she did not want him to see her.

Her arm relaxed involuntarily, and the bag she was carrying rustled. At once Rory said,

'Is that you, Deirdre?'

'Y . . . yes. I . . . I'm sorry I'm late.' She forced herself to move, and carried the groceries over to the cupboard beside the sink. She put them down on top of it, then went over to stand beside him. 'What are you doing?' she asked.

'I've been finding out if I can still load a camera with film,' he replied easily. 'After several tries I finally made it. Watch.'

Relief flowed through her. He couldn't see yet. She felt suddenly weak, and sat down in one of the other chairs and leaned her elbows on the table to watch him.

The frost-scarred hands worked deftly and accurately as he removed the film he had inserted, placed it back in position and closed the camera again. Rory leaned back in his chair, a faint smile curving his mouth. He seemed very pleased with himself, yet Deirdre had the impression of a wariness about him which had not been noticeable before, as if he were waiting for some special reaction from her.

'Unfortunately I can't see to tell when it's indicating that the film is exposed, nor can I take a photograph,' he said with a sigh of frustration. 'God knows when I'll be able to do that. Seems sometimes as if it'll be never.'

The desperation was there, but under better control than it had been, as if the hawk was coming to terms with its imprisonment.

'Please don't say that! I'm sure you'll be able to see sooner than you think,' she told him consolingly.

'And will you be glad when I can, Deirdre?' he asked softly, and she gave him a glance of alarm. Had he been able to guess at her thoughts when she was standing in the kitchen doorway? Guilt made her quiver again and she stood up quickly, trying to stifle it.

'Of course I'll be glad,' she said. 'I'll get the supper ready now.'

She went over to the cupboard and began to unpack the groceries and put them away.

'What's the matter?' he demanded sharply. He must have sensed that she was perturbed after all. 'You sound upset about something. Where have you been until now? It must be quite late.'

'Almost half-past six. I've been at Darroch House—I met Dougal on the road. It was pouring with rain, so I gave him a lift and he invited me in to meet his mother. She's very nice and would like to see you. The twins were there and they want to see you too. They want to know about your accident. You won't mind if they come and ask you about it, will you?'

She seemed to be babbling like the burn, filling the space

81

with noisy speech, not wanting him to think she was upset about anything.

'No, I won't mind,' he said. 'Is Jean at the house?'

'No, she's cruising with her husband. But there was another woman there called Kirsty, who knows you.'

She emptied sugar into an airtight container, waiting for him to reply and admit that he had been on the island five years ago. When he did speak she almost dropped the container. He was right behind her, and she hadn't heard him leave the table and move across the room.

'Kirsty who? I don't remember her,' he said.

She turned to face him. He was standing with his hands in his trouser pockets and was frowning the days of sunshine had given his face a smooth golden tan so that he no longer had the pallid look of illness. Under the slanting eyebrows his eyes did not seem blind between narrowed lids, and she stepped back a pace, a little unnerved to find him so near and yet not be able to gauge his mood.

'Oh, Rory,' she said with a nervous laugh, 'do you go through life forgetting everyone you've ever met?'

He lifted his shoulders and his frown went as he grinned in appreciation of her remark.

'Not on purpose, but I have trouble remembering names. You'll have to describe the woman. What does she look like?' he replied.

He looked brash and lively, more like the person she had met at Toni's party; wild as a hawk, free as the wind, not needing anyone to care for him, not needing someone like herself. The impression was strong and kept her silent, struggling with seething emotions.

'Deirdre, are you still there?' he asked sharply.

'You know I am! You can hear me breathing, and I can't get past you. I'm jammed up against the dresser in the corner,' she countered, and again his grin flashed tauntingly.

'I didn't mean physically, but mentally. Your thoughts were wandering.'

She felt her skin prickle with fear. Could blindness

sharpen a person's extra-sensory perceptions as well as the usual senses of touch, hearing, taste and smell?

'I was thinking how well you look,' she parried hastily. 'You're quite tanned, and you're not as thin as you were.'

'I wondered when you'd notice,' he drawled enigmatically. 'It's all due to that good food you've been giving me, plus the fresh air. All I need now is your company at night, and possibly I'll sleep better too.'

He had every right to make the suggestion: after all, he was her husband, and she had married him unconditionally. Even so, shock ran through her like fire through dry grass and she remained silent and big-eyed, pressed back against the dresser as far from him as possible.

'I gather from your silence that you're not used to the idea yet,' he said drily. 'All right, then, tell me about this Kirsty woman and maybe I'll remember her.'

He moved away from her and once again her breath came out in a gasp of relief. She began to unpack more groceries as she described Kirsty; slim and neat, with shapely hands and feet, glossy hair and a peach-like skin, and the knowledgeable eyes of a mature, confident woman. The sort of woman who might appeal to Rory, who had a passion for beauty.

'You should remember her, because she's beautiful,' she said slowly. She had her back to him and again he gave her a surprise by coming up behind her and curving his hands about her waist. At once she stiffened in reaction to his touch, but this time he didn't move away.

'A woman doesn't have to be physically beautiful for me to remember her,' he said as his hands slipped across her waist and his arms closed about her and drew her back against him. Still and stiff in that embrace, her heart leapt in her breast making her short of breath as she felt the hard line of his jaw against her temple and the vibrant warmth of his body against her back.

'Besides,' he continued softly, 'beauty shows itself in different ways, and in the most unexpected places. It's then that it's more noticeable and worth remebering. You have beautiful hair, I've felt it, and you have beautiful skin. I can feel that too.' He rubbed his cheek against hers and she closed her eyes in an effort to ignore a searing, flamelike sensation which leapt through her body and made her feel slightly giddy. 'And you have a beautiful voice, deep and resonant, like the sound of a cello,' he added. 'What more beauty does a blind man need?'

'Do you remember Kirsty?' she asked. Not much beauty in her voice now. It sounded strangled as she forced herself to remain unperturbed by the murmuring huskiness of his voice and the nerve-tingling touch of his hands.

'Yes, but I don't want to.'

'Why?'

'Are we going to have any supper tonight? I'm hungry. *I* wasn't out to tea. I didn't have any of Margot Fairlie's drop scones,' he evaded easily.

'That doesn't answer my question, and anyway how can I get a meal ready when you're holding me like this?' she retorted.

'You have a point there,' he conceded with a laugh, and released her. 'I'll let you go for now, but don't think for a minute that you're going to escape from me for ever.'

That warning stayed with her all the time she was preparing the meal. She knew now that he had noticed her stiffness and her withdrawal, and she guessed that the time for getting used to each other was over. With the return of his health there was a return of his vigour and a sharpening of all his appetites.

And Deirdre could not really understand herself for withdrawing, she thought as she sat at the table with him later. Although he was blind he was not repulsive. In fact his uncompromising masculinity, the hardness of his lean body and the strength of his hands, the rough-hewn angularity of his face beneath the rust-brown hair, made him very attractive. Letting him make love to her should have come as a natural culmination of their working together in harmony during the day.

But it hadn't happened that way, and she knew why it

had not happened; she wanted him to be in love with her. She wanted him to say he loved her. She did not wish to be used as a substitute for Toni.

And now new suspicions were buzzing in her mind like a swarm of angry hornets, giving her no peace.

'Why didn't you tell me you came here five years ago?' she asked suddenly, and saw him stiffen warily.

'I didn't think you'd be interested in what I was doing five years ago,' he said coolly, 'I didn't want to know what you were doing. We were both different people then, we didn't even know of each other's existence. What can it possibly matter now?'

'Five years ago I was almost eighteen and I'd just finished school,' she murmured, thinking that if she told him a little about herself he might be tempted to reply in kind.

He leaned back in his chair and thrust his hands in his pockets. His mouth twitched with amusement.

'I can just imagine you in a gym tunic and knee-socks, with your hair in a pigtail,' he scoffed.

'We didn't wear gym tunics, we wore pleated navy skirts and white blouses and long beige stockings,' she retorted spiritedly, then added with a rueful smile, 'But you're right, I did have my hair braided.'

'I expect you think it's my turn now to tell you what I was doing,' he jeered. 'Well, I was twenty-nine, nearly thirty, and I'd just held my first exhibition of photographs. Some of them I'd taken the previous year in the Alps where I'd done some climbing—it had taken me nearly ten years to achieve my ambition, and I was exultant and possibly unbearable as a result.'

Encouraged by his attempt to please her with his half-mocking account of his own activities, Deirdre continued with her own memories.

'I was waiting for the results of examinations to find out if I'd be able to go to university. I had a summer job in the baker's shop in the High Street, and I used to love the smell of the bread baking, and the sight of the hot loaves all golden and dusted with flour when they came on trays from the oven. There were lovely cakes too, especially on Saturdays. Éclairs oozing cream, custard slices with vanilla icing on flaky pastry, Neapolitan squares, pink and white, almond slices, coconut macaroons. . . .'

'Stop it,' he ordered, laughing, 'you're making my mouth water. Did you eat many of them?'

'When I was able to buy any of them. I still do.'

'And that's why you're plump,' he accused softly, and she caught her breath to stare at him as her memory winged back to the way he had held her against him earlier. Oh, yes, he would know by now that she wasn't thin. 'Why don't you try making some of those cakes? I wouldn't mind tasting your efforts,' he added.

'I . . . I'm not sure that I could make them,' she stammered pushed off balance by his suggestion. 'I'd have to have the recipes.'

'There should be a recipe book in the place somewhere—Aunt Grace used to make cakes when I stayed with her. Or Margot Fairlie might have a book. Why not ask her?'

'Yes, I will,' she replied. She felt subdued. He had spoken to her as if she were still eighteen, and had to be found something to do to keep her busy and prevent her from being too curious about him. 'You don't want to tell me why you came to t'   five years ago, do you?' she blurted, realizing her h... ... had failed and resorting to direct attack.

He tilted his chair back dangerously on to two legs. She wanted to warn him against this habit, but decided against speaking because she had learned during the past week that he did not like being told not to do something just because it was dangerous or because he couldn't see.

'I've no objection to telling you *why*, if you really must know,' he replied with an air of indulgence, 'I thought it was time I came to see the place. Some years had passed since Aunt Grace had died and left it to me. I hadn't been able to come. I'd been too busy taking photographs, establishing a reputation. Does that satisfy your curiosity?' His voice deepened with sarcasm, warning her that he was

86

becoming irritated with her.

'How long did you stay here?'

'About a month. How long did you work in the baker's shop?' he countered acidly.

'Kirsty said that Sorcha Fairlie left the island the day after you did, that she went to Glasgow and was killed crossing the road on the way to the station,' she said quickly before she could change her mind.

Rory closed his eyes tightly, and his mouth thinned in a long taut line of pain. His cheeks hollowed darkly so that momentarily he looked ill again. The chair tipped forward on to its front legs and he leaned both elbows on the table and rested his head on his hands so that they hid most of his face.

'What else did she tell you?' he asked gruffly.

'That she was a close friend of Sorcha's and that Sorcha followed you.'

He was silent, but she could tell by the way his long fingers grasped at his hair that he was disturbed.

'So that's the way it goes,' he said at last, as if speaking to himself.

'Was she following you?' she asked urgently, wanting desperately for him to deny the insinuation that he had enticed Dougal's wife away.

He raised his head sharply as if to look at her, and his blurred eyes gave him a secretive, sphinx-like expression.

'Maybe she was, but not because I asked her to,' he replied in an icy keep-off-the-grass voice. 'Is it still raining?' he added more normally, and Deirdre acknowledged ruefully that the subject of Sorcha was forbidden territory.

'No. It's still very dull and cloudy,' she said with a sigh.

'While you were out I was thinking we could black out the window in the bedroom and make a darkroom to print some of the negatives. I'd like to find out what the photographs are like before going on with the narrative.' Rory rose to his feet. 'We could print some this evening if you haven't anything else you want to do.'

'No, I haven't anything else to do.'

The window in the bedroom, like all of those in the cottage, was small and set into the thick stone wall so that it had a deep embrasure, and it was easy to cover the panes with a piece of thick cardboard so that no light entered. With the electric light on, Deirdre set up the enlarger on the desk and plugged it in. Then, following Rory's instructions, she mixed the developing and fixing solutions needed for the printing and put them in separate shallow trays.

She felt nervous while she was working, not only because she knew the quality of the prints would depend on how well she followed his instruction, but also because she guessed he was annoyed with her. He was probably regarding her as a naïve, immature nuisance with all her questions about his past, and she had to admit that probably a more sophisticated woman would have closed her eyes to anything he had done at one time and would have accepted him as he was now.

Toni wouldn't have asked questions. Toni would have entertained him with sparkling conversation instead of talking about what she had done five years ago. Toni wouldn't have stiffened and pulled away from him when he had taken her in his arms. Toni would have. . . .

'Deirdre,' his voice was sharp, 'stop daydreaming. That print should be ready now.'

The first print was a beautiful coloured picture of a snow-covered ridge of rock shimmering under sunlight and slashed with deep ravines of indigo blue, that soared up against a cobalt blue sky. At the sight of it Deirdre gasped with delight and admiration, forgetting her suspicions. From then on she worked diligently and methodically, looking forward to the emergence of each print from the fixing solution and making excited comments of admiration about each one to Rory.

But when she saw the print showing two men roped together and climbing a sheer vertical wall of rock, she was silent, thinking of Rory and his friend Euan. They had been

88

climbing like that when Euan had slipped and fallen and they had both gone sliding downwards several hundred feet; one to his death, the other to suffer agonies of frostbite and exposure.

She described each picture to him and he identified them, then she labelled them carefully and placed them in a wire tray until they would be required.

It was inevitable, as they worked together in subdued red light of the photographic light bulb which replaced the usual bedroom light, that they should become more and more aware of each other. Tension built up as it had every evening, and to ease it Deirdre began to chatter about her visit to Darroch House that afternoon, little realising how often she mentioned Dougal's name.

At last Rory called a halt and said it was time to clear away the equipment. Deirdre collected up the trays of chemical solutions, intending to take them into the kitchen, and turned towards the door.

A little shock ran through her. Rory was standing in front of the closed door, leaning against it with his arms folded across his chest. There was something arrogant about his indolent posture which alerted her. It was if he were deliberately blocking her way of escape.

Then she realised that he might not know he was standing in front of the door.

'You like Douglas, don't you?' he said casually.

'Yes, I do. He's very kind and gentle. He's going to show me how to fish so that I can help you, and he says he'd like to show me the standing stones and the caves. . . .'

'I suppose you're sorry for him because his wife was killed?' he interrupted harshly, and not for the first time she wished she could read his face.

'Yes, I am. I think he has problems with his little boy. The child is strange.'

'Oh, in what way?' He sounded interested.

'It's hard to explain. He gave me the impression of being only partially here, as if he knew of another world which we don't know about. Do you know what I mean, Rory?'

89

'I think so. Maybe he's fey like his mother was.'

'Fey? What does that mean?'

'Fated to die.' There was a curious sad note in his husky voice, 'or it can mean disordered in mind.'

'I see.' That could be the explanation for Sorcha's flight from the island five years ago, and perhaps now that Rory had opened the subject of Sorcha again she could ask him more. But first she had to get rid of the trays.

'You're standing in front of the door,' she said tentatively, not liking to remind him of his blindness.

'Am I? That's good, because I intended to stand in front of it,' he replied lightly, not moving an inch.

'Why?' Deirdre's eyes widened.

'To stop you from leaving the room, of course.' His mouth curled a little at one corner, as if he wanted to laugh.

'Oh, please move, Rory! I want to take the solution trays into the kitchen and I'd like to go to bed. We've worked quite hard this evening and I feel tired.'

'You could sleep in here, I've no objections. In fact I think it's time you did,' he said quietly.

The trays rattled together as her hands shook. Tall and taunting, he continued to lean against the door, and his grin mocked her as he sensed her agitation.

'Now why should I want to sleep in here?' she retorted, doing her best to seem cool and collected.

'Don't you know?' he enquired jeeringly. 'To keep me company, of course. I'd have thought someone like you, who is so keen on doing everything properly as long as it's all legal and above board, would know the rules of the marriage game. Perhaps it's time I gave you a few lessons.'

'Let's go and make some tea and talk about it,' she suggessted.

'We've done nothing but talk for over a week and I'm tired of talking.' He paused, then added more seriously, 'You didn't really think I'd be satisfied with a wife in name only, did you?'

'No, I didn't.' Her cheeks were suddenly very hot, and she went to the desk and set down the trays. There didn't seem to be much point in holding them since he wasn't going to let her through the door.

'Then do you think you've been playing fair since we came here?' he asked steadily.

She looked at him. There was no mercy in the set of his mouth and again she had the uneasy feeling that he could see her clearly; that she was no longer a vague dark grey shape against a lighter grey background that he had trapped her in here purposely to force a confrontation on an issue she had been trying to avoid.

'I'm sorry,' she began, and saw his mouth twist with impatience and remembered belatedly that he had once warned her to stop saying she was sorry for everything. 'I thought, I hoped . . . oh, Rory, I know you don't love me and. . . .'

'Love!' The word was an explosion. 'What are you talking about now? Look, Deirdre, I don't go in for white-washing things and trying to make them seem different from what they are, so I don't know what you've been expecting me to do say or do to fit in with some fancy notion you have of what marriage should be. But I do know that you've pulled away from me every time I've touched you this past week, as if . . . as if. . . .' He broke off, his face stiffening with pride. 'I may be blind,' he continued in a steadier voice, 'but I'm not made of cardboard. I have feelings and needs. I've waited fairly patiently for you, hoping you'd get used to living with me, but I think I've waited long enough. Now it's time for action.'

He groped for the light switch on the wall by the door, found it, flicked it off and the room was plunged into darkness.

'Oh, you've put the light off,' gasped Deirdre, trying to peer through the pitch. Now scarcely any light penetrated the room.

'I know I have,' he replied. 'You don't have the advantage any more. You can't see very much. We're as equal as we can possibly me. It should be an interesting game of blind man's buff, now.'

'Please be reasonable,' she pleaded, backing away, convinced that he had stepped towards her.

'Not any more, sweetheart,' and she heard laughter breaking through the huskiness of his voice.

As she backed away she collided with something, and reaching a hand behind her she felt the brass rail of the bed end. A plan of escape leapt into her mind. Feeling along the rail, she moved as quietly as possible, thinking that if she could reach the side of the bed furthest away from the doorway, she could climb over the bed as he followed her. A quick dash across the room and she could be through the door and into the kitchen almost before he realised what had happened. It all depended on whether she could coax him to follow her.

'I didn't mean to cheat you,' she said softly, 'I just thought it would take longer for us to get used to each other. After all, we hardly knew one another before we got married. And I'm so inexperienced. . . .' She was talking rapidly now, saying anything as she moved round the end of the bed, hoping that he was following her.

She reached the side of the bed, clambered on to it and shuffled on her knees to the other side. Rory hadn't spoken, but she could hear his breathing.

She scrambled off the bed and darted towards what she hoped was the door, then bumped into solid bone and muscle. Just over six feet of them.

'Caught you!' he whispered, and put an arm round her to hold her against him in a vice-like grip, crushing the breath out of her. As she tried to struggle free she felt the muscles tighten in his arm, and knew that this time she would be unable to pull away. 'It was a good try, sweetheart, but you're not as good at listening as I am.'

With his free hand he felt over her in the age-old way of blind man's bluff. Up over her breast to her throat and chin the long fingers moved, leaving a trail of nerve-tingling sensations which had the effect of softening any stiffness in her so that her body, as malleable suddenly as putty, wanted to mould itself against his. The fingers traced her mouth caressingly, slid teasingly up the curve of her nose, lingered tenderly on each of her eyelids and stroked her brow soothingly, then slipped slowly over her head as if to savour the silky feel of every strand of hair. They stopped, as she knew they would, at the knot at the nape of her neck. A quick experienced flick of his fingers, and the mass of her hair fell her dislike of his possessive attitude.

'I seem to have caught quite a hefty chunk of woman,' he teased, as if continuing with the game of blind man's bluff. So closely was he holding her that she could feel suppressed laughter shaking his chest. That laughter did something to her; it aroused a fury within her. How dare he treat her like this? How dare he behave as if she were some form of entertainment provided for his sole use? She wanted to beat him with her clenched fists; to convey in some physical way hr dislike of his possessive attitude.

But she couldn't move her arms because they were pinned to her sides. She could only show resistance by keeping her head down stubbornly, her brow against his chest, when he put his fingers under her chin to raise it.

'I didn't think you were the sort of man who would force a woman to submit to your will,' she challenged in a low fierce voice, and felt a flash of triumph as he stiffened in reaction.

'I'm not,' he retorted, 'nor are you the sort of woman who'd submit to force. You'd fight to the last ditch rather than give in, wouldn't you?'

'Yes, I would,' she replied hotly. 'Then why are you holding me like this? If you're not using force to hang on to me, I'd like to know what you are doing.'

'It's all part of the game,' he murmured softly. 'When I asked you to marry me I assumed you'd know the rules and would keep them, but it seems that I was mistaken. You're so prim and proper, so well educated, that you don't understand them and don't recognise your own needs either. Perhaps it's time someone showed you what they are. Better for me to show you than anyone else, and I'm sure you'll agree when I remind you that I'm your husband.'

Strange, tempestuous feelings were threatening to swamp her, and she struggled desperately to keep her head. If she didn't escape from that hard embrace soon, he would be able to do what he wanted with her.

'If you don't let me go—' she began and then paused, searching wildly for a threat to use against him.

'What will you do, sweetheart?' he jeered.

'Don't call me that!'

'Why not?'

'I . . . I don't know. Oh, it makes me feel as if I'm one of many!'

'One of many what?' he queried. 'I agree it's a misnomer while you're in your present mood, there's nothing sweet about you at the moment. But then a little spice often sharpens the appetite. What will you do if I don't let you go?'

'I'll hate you for ever,' she cried desperately, already hating him for making fun of her.

He clicked his tongue mockingly.

'Tut, tut, how violent you're becoming! How you swing from one extreme to the other. Love and hate—and you're fond of those words *for ever*. I never use them myself, I'm interested in now, and for the time being you're my wife; not anyone else's, but *mine*.'

The open possessiveness of his words, the sheer arrogance of it, sent a thrill of excitement through her even while her intelligence rejected it. Was she no better than a romancing adolescent? Was she going to allow herself to be bowled over by a show of masculine tyranny?

Once again she made an effort to assert absolute control by mind over matter, only to find that her senses were being led into open rebellion by the touch of his fingers as they wandered casually down from her chin to explore the hollow of her throat, left bare by the unbuttoned collar of her shirt. Lower still they drifted, gently seductive against the V of warm skin.

'You've a lot to learn yet, my puritan,' he whispered, 'but I can guarantee it won't always be against your will. There are other ways besides force.'

At that Deirdre raised her head to make one last stand against him to stave off the utter destruction of her defences against him.

'Now, you're not playing fair,' she accused.

She wasn't able to say any more because he seized the advantage again, pressing his mouth against hers in a ruthless demand. Something exploded in her head like a charge of dynamite, and after that she had no control over anything that she did.

CHAPTER SIX

THE sound of a voice calling awakened Deirdre, and she lay on her stomach with her eyes closed and listened for the voice again, not sure whether she had really heard it or whether it had been part of a dream.

It came again, clear and cool, strangely sexless. It could belong either to a woman or to a boy whose voice had not broken: it was quite near, and it was calling her name. It was calling for Rory, too.

Deirdre opened her eyes cautiously as she had done every morning for the past few days. Slowly she looked sideways along the white expanse of pillow to the next pillow, surprise ran through her and her eyes opened wider. There was no head crowned by ruffled rust-brown hair lying on that other pillow, as there had been every other morning this week. That side of the bed was empty.

Then where was Rory?

Realising that sunlight was bright and yellow on the walls, she twisted over and sat up. The room looked a little as if a high wind had swept through it, as in his effort to find clothing for himself Rory had left the wardrobe door hanging open and drawers in the dresser, pulled out. Some papers from the desk had also drifted to the floor.

The door of the room was slightly open and through it she heard the voice calling again quite loudly. She guessed that the person who was calling had opened the door into the hallway.

'Cooeeee, Deirdre, Rory! Anyone at home? It's time to get up!'

Recognising the voice as belonging to Kirsty, Deirdre leaned over to glance guiltily at her watch on the bedside table. It was past ten o'clock; she had overslept. Why hadn't Rory wakened her as he had every morning recently?

Cheeks burning at the thought of those awakenings, she waited for him to answer Kirsty's call, but there was no reply from the kitchen. Then she wondered why Kirsty had come. When no one had come to visit from Darroch House, she had begun to think that there was some truth in Kirsty's allegation that Dougal held Rory responsible for Sorcha's death, and that this kept everyone from visiting the cottage.

But where was Rory now?

In a strange sort of panic in case he had gone out on his own and had possibly tripped and fallen somewhere, she jumped out of bed and went to the door to speak to Kirsty. At that moment she heard the woman step outside again, and heard the clear fluting voice say,

'Hello there, Rory Mallon. It's no use pretending it isn't you behind those dark glasses. I'd recognise the height and breadth of you, and your russet hair, anywhere.'

Dark glasses! Deirdre closed the bedroom door and began to look for her discarded clothing. Rory hadn't worn the glasses to protect his eyes since they had arrived on the island; he had said he hadn't felt any need for them. Then why was he wearing them this morning? Was it because he was conscious of sun glare?

'And I'd recognise that clarion call of yours anywhere, Kirsty Brown,' Rory shouted back as he approached the house. 'What are you doing here?'

'I've come to visit you and your wife, that is if she's still here,' replied Kirsty. 'What have you done with her? I've called several times without any luck. Has she left you already?'

There it was again, that needling, suggestive manner of Kirsty's which insinuated all the time, taunting and troublemaking.

'No, not yet,' Rory sounded amused. 'Do you expect her to leave me?'

'Well, she seemed quite glad to have escaped from you for a few hours the other day when Douglas brought her home with him.' Kirsty's voice carried quite clearly through the open window. 'It was really rather funny,' she continued with a superior little laugh, 'she was all damp and straggly like an overgrown long-haired puppy tossed out into the rain. I think Dougal was a little sorry for her, and that's why he invited her in; you know what he's like. Anyone who seems hurt or mistreated in any way always make a big appeal to him. That's why he married Sorcha.'

Deirdre found she was fighting an urge to lower the window even further, stick her head out of it and shout,

'Don't listen to her, Rory. It's not true. Dougal wasn't sorry for me, he had no need to be.'

Shaking a little, she searched for a clean shirt, hearing the door into the house open and the murmur of voices as Rory and Kirsty went into the kitchen. She had just found the shirt when the bedroom door opened and Rory stepped into the room. He closed the door behind him and leaned against it, and at the sight of him, tall and muscular in cream sweater and dark trousers, his hair wind-tossed, the dark glasses giving him a cool withdrawn look, it struck her that even after all that had happened between them he was still a tantalising stranger. She had no idea of what went on in his mind, nor could she predict what he would do or say next.

'Deirdre? Are you up?' he said quietly.

'Yes, I'm getting dressed. You should have woken me. Where have you been?'

'Walking. I went as far as the burn.'

It was the first time he had gone out alone since they had come to the island. Unaccountably she felt jealousy stir within her, because he had chosen to go without her.

'Do you think you should have gone by yourself?' she asked. 'The ground is uneven, and you could have tripped over a rock and hurt yourself. Or you could have walked into the water.'

'And I didn't do either, mother hen,' he jeered softly. 'You have a very poor opinion of my abilities. We've gone that way so often I know it by heart.'

Moving away from the door, he came towards her. She tried to shrink away, but could not avoid his hands as they reached out to her shoulders; they were cool from his walk and she caught her breath as they touched her warm skin. She saw his eyebrows lift mockingly.

'I thought you were dressed,' he said.

'I am, nearly, but I haven't put my shirt on. What does Kirsty want?'

'So you did hear her! Why didn't you answer her?'

'I was going to, when I heard her speaking to you?'

She held herself stiffly, trying to ignore a desire to nestle against him, trying not to show the effect the subtle caress of his fingers on her shoulders had on her. Recently she had learned why she had always been afraid of him touching her, for he had the power to destroy her control over her senses and emotions.

'Holding out on me, as usual?' he scoffed softly as he noticed her stiffness. 'Why?'

'You know why,' she retorted. 'It's still against my will.' His mouth made a curve of derision.

'That's what you *think*,' he drawled, 'but not what you *feel*. How long are you going to deceive yourself? Oh, I know you like to pretend you don't like me to assert my rights as your husband, but you don't deceive me. You like to be caught and kissed.'

The new fiery feeling which Deirdre was learning to live with blazed up within her. As if he sensed it, he moved

98

away from her and went to lean against the desk, his arms folded across his chest and that faint derisive smile still flickering about his mouth.

The fiery feeling died down, leaving her with a cold ache. Rory was moving about more confidently—as if he could see properly, she thought—and when he could see again he wouldn't need her.

Up, then down. Hot, then cold. This see-sawing of her emotions made her feel exhausted. She understood herself no longer.

'Kirsty has come over with an invitation; we've been invited to go on a picnic. Would you like to go?' he said coolly.

'Would you?' she asked rather foolishly, and pulled on her shirt.

He shrugged his shoulders noncommittally.

'I thought it might make a change for you,' he drawled, 'you must be getting tired of being cooped up here, and bored with listening to me talking about the Mountains of Kumoa.'

'Oh, no,' she denied urgently, 'I'm not tired, or not bored with the work we've been doing. I've loved every minute of it.'

'Kirsty also says that Dougal is thinking of taking the twins and Alan for a walk over to the other side of the island, and that you're invited to join them. They'd be leaving before noon and taking a picnic lunch with them.'

'I . . . I couldn't go without you,' she faltered.

'I don't see why not, there isn't any point in me going. I wouldn't be able to walk over rough ground without being led every step of the way.' Rory's face was grim.

'Would you object if I led you?' she offered, feeling another warm surge of compassion for his helplessness. Oh, why was every feeling she experienced the result of anything he did or said? It seemed as if her emotions were his slaves, to be manipulated as he wished.

'Yes, I would,' he replied curtly.

'But you haven't objected when we've walked to the

burn.'

'That's different. We've been by ourselves. This would be in front of others, and I've no wish to flounder about in front of them.'

'You don't flounder. You walk very well, and anyway they'd understand.'

'They're not going to get the chance,' he said tautly, and she sighed as she recognised she was up against that stubborn pride of his which made him hate appearing helpless in public.

'But if you'd like to see something of the island you should go with them,' he continued more calmly. 'Think about it while you're getting dressed, and then come and tell Kirsty yourself.' He paused at the door and half-turned towards her. 'She seems to think you want to run away from me. I wonder what gave her such an idea?' he said.

'I wonder?' she replied as coolly as she could, and could not help feeling relieved when he opened the door and went from the room without asking any more questions.

She finished fastening her shirt and tucked it into the waistband of her skirt, then she went to the mirror to fix her hair. She had given up wearing it in a bun; after Rory had pulled it down several times during a day there didn't seem to be any reason for binding it up. Hanging loosely about her face it made her look different, less serious, more feminine. Changed.

But then she was changing, slowly, inexorably. Gone was the old Deirdre, the calm, self-contained girl who had come to terms with loneliness early in life and had really thought she did not need anyone for company, least of all a man like Rory Mallon. Her place was being taken by a woman whose emotions swung violently, so that sometimes she wanted nothing more in life than to belong to Rory and be loved by him, and at other times she longed to run away from him so that she could become once again that cool unawakened girl, impervious to passion.

She sighed, picked up a ribbon, flung her hair back and gathered it in at the nape of her neck, and tied the ribbon round it. She thought she looked a little pale, but her eyes had deep green glow and her mouth had a bruised look as if it had been kissed many times. When she lowered her arm she noticed with a gasp of dismay dark finger-marks where Rory had caught and held it once, when she tried to escape from him. So she rolled down the sleeve of her shirt and fastened the cuff. She did not want those critical blue eyes of Kirsty's to see too much.

On her way to the kitchen she paused in the little hall-way, because she could hear Kirsty talking in a gentle, con-solatory way.

'I was so sorry to hear about Euan's death. You must miss him terribly,' she was saying, 'as I miss Sorcha. She and I were such good friends. We had no secrets from each other. We told each other everything. *Everything*, Rory.'

'Did you? That must have been very interesting for you both.' Rory was being lightly ironic in the way he could be if he was heartily bored by the conversation.

'I suppose you realise Dougal knows. That's why he hasn't come to see you.'

'Knows what?' Now Rory sounded wearily disgusted. 'Why the hell can't you ever say anything straight? Why do you always have to drop hints?'

How like him to say what he thought honestly, thought Deirdre with a little grin, wishing she could see how Kirsty had reacted.

'He knows where Sorcha was going when she was killed,' said Kirsty importantly.

'So?' That one word, insolently spoken, was meant to be a deterrent. But Kirsty was not to be deterred.

'She was going to meet you,' she asserted triumphantly.

'Was she? Where?' Rory sounded bored again. 'And where did Douglas get the idea she had gone to meet me?'

'Remembering all that happened here five years ago, it wouldn't be difficult for him to put two and two together, would it?' snapped Kirsty, obviously becoming irritated by his coolness.

'Since he wasn't here half the time that summer, how

could he know what happened unless someone told him?' Rory's tone was mocking and Deirdre, hearing Kirsty make an exclamation of irritation, decided it was time she went into the kitchen and rescued the woman from his merciless treatment.

'Hello, Kirsty. Sorry I wasn't up when you called,' she said brightly, going into the room.

Kirsty's eyes were glittering angrily and her cheeks were bright pink, and she had obviously just stood up to make her departure. Rory was leaning back in a chair by the table, the dark glasses making it difficult to read the expression on his face, but Deirdre recognised the taunting curve to his mouth.

'Hello, Deirdre. I've brought Margot's apologies for not having been down to see you and Rory, but she still has the feeling that a honeymoon shouldn't be interrupted,' said Kirsty.

'Pity you don't feel that way too,' taunted Rory.

'Rory, please,' Deirdre appealed and saw him grin unrepentantly before she turned to Kirsty. 'I'd like to go for that picnic with Dougal and the twins, and stay to tea later. What time are they setting off?'

'About eleven-thirty, Dougal said,' Kirsty replied sullenly.

'Then I'll come up about eleven-fifteen. Will that be all right?' asked Deirdre.

'Just you?' exclaimed Kirsty. 'Aren't you coming, Rory?'

'No, thanks. I'd rather stay put until I can see properly. It would be a waste of time for me to go on a picnic,' he replied evenly.

'And you'll let Deirdre come by herself?' Kirsty sounded slightly shocked.

'I'm her husband, you know, not her jailer,' retorted Rory. 'If Deirdre wishes to go, she's free to do so.'

'Oh, very well. It's up to you entirely,' said Kirsty, who seemed very put out by the idea.

'I'm glad you realise that,' returned Rory drily, and

Kirsty gave him a vindictive glance which was absolutely wasted on him because he couldn't see it.

'I find it rather odd, considering what happened five years ago, that you'll let your wife go anywhere without you,' said Kirsty waspishly. 'However I suppose you know what you're doing.'

'I think I do,' retorted Rory through gritted teeth. Goodbye, Kirsty.'

Deirdre followed Kirsty into the porch, but as she was about to go through the door she turned.

'You ought to make him come,' she said crisply.

'He doesn't want to, and. . . .'

'You should assert yourself,' Kirsty swept on, 'make him come with you. Otherwise you shouldn't come without him and go walking with Dougal—it isn't right. People will only think the worst. I can see you're far too young to deal with a man like Rory, he should have married an older woman, someone less soft and gentle, not so easily trampled on, someone. . .'

'Like yourself, perhaps?' Deirdre spoke out of sudden anger, but to her surprise Kirsty looked pleased.

'Possibly, possibly. He might have been interested in me, too, five years ago, if it hadn't been for Sorcha.'

'I don't believe you!' Deirdre exclaimed.

'Don't you?' Kirsty's smile was pitying. 'Poor little innocent! You've a lot to learn yet about him. Never think for one moment you've been the only woman in his life.'

'I've never thought that, but I certainly don't believe that you've been one of them, or would ever be.'

Kirsty's eyes flashed, but all she said was:

'Why not ask him why he's afraid to come up to Darroch House today? Ask him if he's avoiding Dougal, and I think you'll find his answer interesting. See you later.'

She went off, swinging gracefully along the road. Deirdre closed the door slowly on the soft sunlit morning and hurried back to the kitchen.

Rory was still there, his elbows on the table. The dark glasses were off and his hands were pressed against his eyes. Deirdre went over to him and laid a hand on his shoulder.

'What's wrong?' she asked softly.

He removed his hands from his eyes, groped for the glasses and put them on, then said curtly,

'Nothing.'

'That's not true. Are your eyes hurting you? You haven't worn the glasses since we came here—in fact I'm surprised you were to find them.'

'Didn't you notice the state of the bedroom?' he queried with a laugh. 'My eyes are all right, I just felt like wearing the glasses. Makes a change from two shades of grey.'

'I wish you'd tell me what's wrong this morning,' she tried again.

'There's nothing wrong,' he retorted irritably.

'Yes, there is. You've never gone out early by yourself before.'

'Miss me?' he whispered tauntingly, and her cheeks grew warm as she recalled the other mornings she had woken in that other room.

'Sometimes it helps to share troubles,' she persisted.

'I don't agree. I prefer to keep mine to myself. I don't see why I should tell you everything.'

'We're married.'

'And does that give you the right to know everything about me?' he challenged. 'Sorry to disillusion you, but it doesn't, no more than it gives me the right to know everything about you. The less we know about each other's past the better.' He laughed suddenly as if delighted by a thought. 'Have you a past, my puritan? I doubt it.'

'I wish you wouldn't call me that,' she retorted.

'Why not? Your attitude to life is remarkably pure and unpolluted. You're a rare specimen in my experience. How else should I describe you. Naïve? Refreshingly innocent. . . .'

'Oh, stop making fun! I know as much as any other woman my age.'

'Do you? I know you're very clever and you have lots of

knowledge stored away in that brain of yours, but it's all second-hand stuff. You've learned it from books, not from living in the true sense of the word. You've been alive and breathing, but you haven't lived until now. Aren't I right?' he challenged.

'Dear me,' she said drily, 'you have got an exaggerated idea of your own importance, haven't you? Just because I haven't lived with you before it doesn't mean to say I haven't lived.'

'But you've no idea what kissing you has been like,' he replied softly, and her knees shook so that she had to sit down suddenly on the nearest chair. 'It's like kissing someone who's been asleep for a hundred years. Now I know how the prince felt in the story of the Sleeping Beauty.'

'Oh!' she gasped. 'And it's becoming more and more obvious to me that you've never read a book in your life, other than fairy tales.'

'I didn't read them. They were read to me by my grandmother,' he replied easily. 'And now that I've told you that exciting snippet from my wild and lurid past, do you think you could get some breakfast ready? Or have you gone on strike today?'

She fled to the stove, where she rattled pans noisily. Now she knew what that new feeling was which blazed up within her so suddenly, it was hate, an emotion she had been brought up to suppress and which she had never allowed herself to feel for anyone.

I'll hate you for ever. That was her own threat, made to try to divert him a few nights ago. And it had come true. She hated him because he could make love to her without being in love with her, because he had kissed her awake from her long sleep and made her aware of desires she had not known she possessed. Because he had reduced her to the status of a slave, brought to submission by the touch of his big frost-scarred hands.

Breakfast was an unusually silent meal as Deirdre sat seething, and when she had cleared away and washed up it was time for her to go to Darroch House. The fire of her

105

hate died down, she turned to Rory impulsively and said,
'I wish you'd come. I don't like leaving you all alone.'
'You're doing it again,' he jeered.
'Doing what?'
'Fussing like a mother hen. I'll be all right.'
'I really can't understand why you won't come. Anyone would suspect you're afraid to meet Dougal,' she said.
'And why should I be afraid to do that?'
She swallowed hard, suddenly afraid to say what she had to say.
'Come on, Deirdre. You can't make such a remark and get away with it,' he rebuked her coldly.
'You're afraid to meet him because you stole his wife away from him,' she said in a thin choked voice.
It was said at last. Suspicion was out in the open, and she felt better for putting it into words.
'I know I don't measure up to those high moral principles of yours,' he said angrily, 'but I haven't stooped to wife-stealing, nor am I afraid to meet Dougal. Is that clear?'
He was standing over her, his hands on his hips, and she wondered if he knew how overpowering his physical presence could be when he stood like that.
'Yes, very clear,' she replied without a tremor, 'but I don't believe you.'
That got through his skin, and he went very pale. His hands shot out, found her shoulders and shook her.
'Why?' he demanded. 'Why won't you believe me?'
'I suppose you think that because I'm your wife I have to believe everything you say?' she said sweetly, in imitation of the way he had spoken to her earlier. 'Sorry to disillusion you, but it doesn't work out like that. Since you deliberately avoid questions and won't tell me anything about yourself, I can only suspect you have something to hide of which you're ashamed.'
There would be finger marks on her shoulders now, she thought ruefully as his hands tightened. His anger had thinned his lips and they curved back over his clenched

teeth. Now he was hating her as she had hated him, and she knew a strange triumph because she had been able to rouse him to such intensity of feeling.

'So what do I have to do to convince you that I'm not afraid of Dougal and didn't steal his wife from him?' he said at last in a gruff, oddly hesitant way.

She raised a hand and laid it flat on his chest. Beneath it she could feel the leap of his heart, still thudding furiously as a result of his anger. Her fingers spread out like a fan. Her hand slid upwards and touched his throat, then traced the firm line of his jaw in a shy caress,

'You could come with me, now,' she said appealingly, and watched his mouth for a change in his attitude. As she had hoped, the taut line softened as he half-smiled.

'Aha, a change of tactics,' he scoffed. 'You're learning. This is the first time you've tried this approach. All right, I'll walk up to the house with you and meet Dougal, but I'm not going on the picnic. Will that do?'

It was better than nothing, but it did not allay her suspicions entirely. She knew now from reading his diary about the ascent of the mountains that he had nerves of steel; meeting a man he had possibly deceived would not necessarily present any problems to him, no matter what Kirsty believed.

But she was glad he was with her as she walked along the road to the house on the headland. On one side the sea shimmered serenely, blue dappled with yellow light, and beyond it the green hills of the mainland played hide-and-seek in a violet haze. On the other side the curving moors were purple-pooled with heather in bloom and as they topped the ridge and looked down on the U-shaped bay, she saw golden-brown cattle grazing contentedly in green pastures sprinkled with yellow mustard flowers.

They approached the house hand in hand, laughing at something he had said, and looking for all the world like two people in love with each other to the eyes of the person who was watching them come.

By the time they reached the front door Margot was out

on the step to greet them, with the twins and Alan close behind her.

'It's lovely to see you after all this time, Rory,' said Margot without any hesitation.

'Hello,' said Geordie, peering up at him curiously, 'are you really blind or are you just having us on?'

There was a funny little pause, and Deirdre felt Rory's hand tighten on hers. Then he was laughing easily and saying,

'That must be one of Jean's twin terrors. Which one?'

'Geordie,' moaned Margot. 'Please excuse him, Rory. Jean never tells them to hold their tongues, and the result is that they say whatever comes into their heads.'

'I'm not completely blind,' said Rory calmly. 'I can see vague shapes. I've been told the shapes will take on colour and detail one day. Itts just a question of being patient.'
and detail one day. It's just a question of being patient.'
Dougal had come out of the house to join them, sidling up rather diffidently as if unsure of how he might be greeted.

'How are you, Doug?' Rory released Deirdre's hand so that he could stretch his right hand in the direction of the voice.

'Fine, just fine,' muttered Dougal, taking the proffered hand in his and shaking it, and Deirdre had the impression that Margot relaxed with relief. 'I thought you weren't coming with us?'

'I'm not coming on the picnic, I just walked along with Deirdre to make sure she arrived here safely.'

They all laughed at the slight irony in his voice.

'You've got all your fingers anyway,' said Geordie, who was still carrying on an investigation. 'It said in the newspaper that you might lose some of them through frostbite.'

Rory held out his hands, spreading the fingers wide.

'Have a good look. How many can you see? As far as I can tell they're all there,' he replied.

Geordie, Beth and Alan crowded round him, like pins drawn to a magnet. Watching him as he talked to them, Deirdre was conscious of a new feeling, a bursting feeling of pride because he was handling the situation far better than she had ever imagined he could. The questions were coming fast and furiously from the twins, and he was answering them carefully and patiently, not shirking the difficult ones about his fall.

Margot touched her on the arm and drew her to one side.

'He looks so well, in spite of everything that happened,' she observed. 'You've done a good job, Deirdre. You've given him something he's never had before and I can see a difference in him. Yet it's still there, that power to attract. Look at the twins, and even wee Alan! I'm sure that if he suggested to them that they climb Beinn an Oir with him this afternoon and stayed the night on its summit, they'd follow him in the same way that Jean and Dougal did. And look at Dougal,' Margot's voice softened to a warm chuckle, 'he's listening and pretending he isn't. He's just as fascinated as the children are.'

Deirdre glanced sideways and smiled. Dougal was leaning against the estate car, stuffing tobacco into the bowl of his pipe, apparently waiting patiently for them to go on the picnic with him. But it was obvious that he was listening closely to every word Rory was saying.

'Can you persuade Rory to stay here with you for the afternoon?' Deirdre asked, turning to Margot. 'I don't like to leave him by himself at the cottage, yet I would like to go on the picnic.'

'I'll be pleased to do that,' said Margot. 'I'm glad he came here with you. I've been afraid. . . .' Margot hesitated, frowned and went on in a low voice, 'I was afraid that what has been said about him was true, that he enticed Sorcha away from here. You see he was capable of doing it, and although I said that I didn't come to see you because you were on your honeymoon, that wasn't my real reason for not calling on you.'

'When you didn't act upon my invitation during the past week I think I realised that,' replied Deirdre, 'you were suspicious, as I've been. You'll be interested to know then that Rory came with me this afternoon to convince me that he isn't afraid to meet Dougal because he didn't entice Sorcha away from him. He didn't ask her to follow him.'

'So everything is all right,' said Margot thankfully.

'Ready to go?' Kirsty's clear voice rang out from the doorway where she had just appeared, neat as ever in navy blue slacks, blue-and-white striped sweater and a bright red scarf tied over her hair.

'Of course we're ready,' said Geordie. 'We're only waiting for you. Rory came here after all—you said he wouldn't.'

'And he's going to stay with me until you all come back,' said Margot, smiling.

'What's all this?' asked Rory.

'Please stay here until I come back,' Deirdre whispered to him, 'then I'll know you're safe.'

'But how will I know you're safe?' he surprised her by whispering back.

'You'll just have to trust me,' she replied, and on sudden impulse reached up to kiss him on the cheek.

CHAPTER SEVEN

A FEW days later, Deirdre sat on a conveniently flat-topped rock and gazed out at the glitter of sunlight on the wide expanse of the Atlantic Ocean. The sea appeared to be flat and smooth like thin silk, stretching away to a silvery haze which marked the edge of the world.

Smiling at little at her own fancy, Deirdre tilted her head back to feel the warmth of the sun on her face, and saw in the high blue sky a reminder that the world was round and that there were other lands beyond that haze. Twin vapour trails left by a west-flying jet plane curved like skeins of curly white wool against the blue; and for a moment he stared at them ,her imagination flying with them to the ever-tempting west.

Then her gaze slid downwards, caught by a movement. Above glinting rocks whose jagged edges seemed to cut into the sky, a big bird circled watchfully, its wide wings stretched out still and flat as it glided on currents of air.

The silence of that place was broken only by the gurgle of swirling water; water so clear that it was possible to see the colour of the stones lying beneath its surface as it washed into a rocky inlet. Then came the high sound of children's voices as they approached over the rocks, and the deeper rumble of Dougal's voice as he answered them.

This was Deirdre's third outing with them, and today Kirsty had not come. Complaining that she had sprained an ankle on a previous walk, she had remained at Darroch House to rest it. Rory was also there, being kept safe by Margot until Deirdre's return.

Deirdre frowned uneasily. Since that first outing of hers, Rory had been different, if she hadn't known he could not see properly, she would have said he was watchful in the same way that the circling eagle was. Watchful, wary and possibly waiting for something to happen. The eagle would wait for its prey to run and then it would go into action, swooping down with its big talons curved and ready.

But what was Rory waiting for? Was he waiting for her to run so that he could reach out and catch her?

'See the eagle?' Dougal had come to join her on her rock.

'Yes. What sort is it?'

'A golden one.' He eyed the bird admiringly.

'Aren't they rare?'

'You'll find them wherever there are red deer, mountain hares and sheep. Although over here in the Hebrides they live on sea-birds too.'

'Monarch of all he surveys,' murmured Deirdre, her glance going to the eagle again.

'Very much so here, where there's no one to challenge him,' replied Dougal. 'Have you seen the seals down in the

111

inlet?'

She glanced down at the inlet. The unmistakable rounded heads of several grey seals bobbed above the surface, and as she watched one of them heaved itself out of the water, and rolled ecstatically on its back in the warm sunshine.

'We have our own two seals which visit the bay near the cottage,' she said. She had found Dougal a pleasant companion on these walks; he had a vast store of knowledge about the island, and she knew she was fortunate to have someone with her who shared her own interest in folklore, history and natural phenomena.

'Have you eved heard them singing in the night?' he asked.

'No, I'm usually alseep then,' she replied with a laugh.

'It's a very eerie sound,' he told her, taking out his pipe and beginning to fill it. 'Like a soul crying in anguish in the dark; a soul which has been locked out from warmth and happiness.'

It wasn't the first time she had been chilled by something he had said. He had a great interest in the supernatural which was perhaps not unusual, to find in the grandson of Alasdair Darroch, but which Deirdre felt was a little unhealthy.

She glanced sideways at him. Melancholy sat like a shadow on his face, emphasizing its harsh lines, and his hands were still as if he had forgotten about hips pipe. He seemed to be gazing at nothing, or perhaps into the past; he looked haunted, and it wasn't hard to guess who haunted him. Sorcha, his dead wife.

'Rory once told me that your grandfather said Darroch hands were still as if he had forgotten about his pipe. He there—he pushed her to her death,' she said casually.

He gave her a surprised glance, then busied himself with his pipe-filling again.

'My grandfather had many such tales to tell,' he shrugged noncommittally.

'Do you believe that one?'

'It isn't hard to believe, especially when you know what it's like to be riven by jealousy, as the woman's husband was supposed to be.'

Riven. A strange, angry word to use. A word which conjured up the splintering sound of something, which had once been whole, being torn apart. Deirdre stared at Dougal, seeing the dark lines carved into his face in a different way, no longer were they lines of patience, but lines put there by hours of agony as he had been tortured by jealousy. Jealousy of Rory?

'Rory was very shocked when he learned of Sorcha's death. You see, he didn't know she was dead.' She felt determined to get to the bottom of this particular mystery once and for all, although she doubted if it was possible without Rory's co-operation.

Again Dougal gave her a surprised glance.

'Somehow I've always felt that he must have known,' he replied slowly.

'How could he know? You didn't tell him, nor did anyone else in your family. None of you wrote to him to tell him, so how could he know?'

He looked nonplussed, his eyes dark and wide as he stared at her. She waited, knowing that it would take a while for his slowly working mind to find an answer to her question.

'I don't know,' he admitted at last. 'I suppose I must have assumed that he was at the scene of the accident, that they'd arranged to meet outside the station and he was waiting for her. I thought that. . . .' he broke off and bowed his head in sudden pain. 'Ach, I've thought many things these past five years.'

'Rory could never be so cruel as to watch her being killed and not get in touch with you! He wasn't there. He didn't know until I told him,' she cried, the words wrenched out of her.

'How do you know he couldn't?' he challenged her. 'Do you know him so well?'

She looked away, biting her lip, unable to explain that it

113

was a feeling she had rather than knowledge.

'Your loyalty lies with him, quite naturally,' Dougal continued, 'he's your husband. Who told you about Sorcha and him?'

'Kirsty. She told me Sorcha was following him.'

Dougal nodded grimly.

'She told me that, too. So you told Rory, and what did he say?'

'He said that Sorcha may have followed him, but not because he asked her to. He said he isn't a wife-stealer, Dougal.'

The sound of the match scraping against the side of the matchbox made a small flaring sound. High and clear came the sound of the children's voices as they played amongst the rocks. Beyond those sounds was the silence of an island inhabited only by a handful of people, wild birds and beasts, and some sheep and cattle.

'He didn't have to ask her,' said Dougal slowly. 'Rory just had to be . . . to exist.'

The pipe lit and he puffed at it, staring out at the shining silken sea.

'I . . . I'm not sure I know what you mean,' said Deirdre.

Dougal stared at the glowing bowl of his pipe, as if trying to find a way of explaining more fully what he meant.

'You remember when he came with you to the house a few days ago?' he asked at last.

'Yes, I do,' she nodded.

'And you saw what happened? You saw the way the children crowded round him, as if drawn to a magnet?'

'Not just the children. You too,' she teased, and his twisted smile mocked himself.

'Me too,' he admitted reluctantly, 'I know I'm no better than anyone else. Even as a boy he had that compelling attraction. It's nothing to do with the way he looks, and nothing to do with what he's done, either. It's something innate, not acquired. You always have the feeling that being with him will make life more worth living; that if you don't go where he leads you'll miss something exciting, and be for

114

ever regretting it. Do you know what I mean, Deirdre?'

'Yes, I know,' she admitted. She thought of Toni, seeing what her friend and Rory had in common, and could be a basis of mutual attraction between them.

'Jean and I used to follow him around as if he were the Pied Piper,' said Dougal, chuckling a little as if he had fond memories of the time he had followed Rory.

'And you believe Sorcha felt that attraction too?' Deirdre asked.

His face grew sombre again.

'I know she did, I saw it happen when they met. We hadn't seen him for years, only heard about him, then he walked in one summer day, right into the kitchen at Darroch House where Sorcha was nursing Alan.' He stopped abruptly, half turning away from her, not wishing to reveal his emotion.

Deirdre shifted her position, her vivid imagination recreating the scene, feeling the shock of that meeting between Sorcha and Rory.

'Once she had laid eyes on him she forgot me. She forgot Alan too,' muttered Dougal. 'I had to go away, and I left Sorcha and Alan here with Jean, the twins and Kirsty. My parents had gone abroad that summer for their holidays, and I thought she would be safe. I should never have gone, or I ought to have taken her with me.'

'Do you think she would have gone with you?' Deirdre asked.

'I have to believe that,' he said stubbornly, turning on her suddenly. 'If I don't ... I might as well admit that I made a mistake when I married her. When I came back I found that she'd left the day before I returned.'

'Did she leave a note for you?'

'No.' His voice was full of pain.

'Don't you find that strange? Women usually go in for leaving notes. They like everyone to know their motives. I suppose you could call it a form of female egotism,' said Deirdre, with a touch of humour.

'But Sorcha was always a little strange, different from

115

others. Although she was the only child of wealthy parents when I first met her, she struck me as being like a deprived child—even though she was twenty-five and the same age as myself. It was as if she had lost someone she had loved very much, and never recovered from the experience. I suppose I was sorry for her.'

'I understand. You married her because you were sorry for her; you felt you could make up her loss.'

'That's right,' he nodded. His dark eyes lit up with a glint of appreciation, as if he found her instinctive understanding comforting. 'And in the process I fell in love with her.'

Deirdre watched Alan, the product of Dougal's love for Sorcha, trying to scramble over the rocks in an attempt to keep up with his cousins.

'Haven't you ever thought of marrying again, to provide a mother for Alan?' she asked. Dougal looked away.

'Yes, I have thought about it, and I would if I could find someone suitable.'

'And you haven't yet?'

'Not until this summer,' he said quietly.

It seemed to Deirdre that a bell sounded in one of her ears; she had heard it before and regarded it always as a warning. *Left for love and right for spite.* The old saying of her mother's came to her mind. The sound was in her right ear. Was someone somewhere being spiteful about her this afternoon?

Then she looked into Dougal's opaque brown eyes, and took fright at what she saw as she realised what he meant. This summer he had found her, and considered her suitable to be stepmother to his little boy. She felt herself recoil like a spring which has been stretched too far, bounding back behind the wall of her reserve, from which her compassion, as usual, had tempted her to reach out.

At that moment Alan, trying to be too adventurous, stumbled and slithered down the rock he had been climbing and let out a yell. Immediately Deirdre was on her feet and running to him. She picked him up and examined the scratches on his knees, talking to him all the time, comforting him by telling him he was like Rory, who had also fallen down a big mountain and had hurt himself. This suggestion appealed to him, and he stopped sobbing to gaze at her with eyes which unshed tears made even brighter.

'It's time we were going back to the car,' said Dougal, coming up to them. 'We'll go back a different way, so that you can see the standing stones, and we might just come across some deer.'

On the walk back across the moors to the place where they had left the estate car, Deirdre made sure she was not left alone with Dougal again; sometimes letting Beth lead her aside to examine a wild flower she had not noticed before, sometimes letting Geordie call her attention to yet another interesting piece of rock which, he was sure, held the fossilized remains of some prehistoric animal.

Yet everywhere she went Alan was with her, and she found herself regretting having comforted him after his fall as he hung on to her hand. In view of Dougal's remark and the way he had looked at her, such attention on the part of his son was embarrassing, but she could do nothing about it without hurting the child's feelings.

They came upon the stag suddenly as they skirted a clump of stunted trees. It had been grazing in a sheltered dell, a mere dip in the moors, and on hearing them it stood poised, its antlered head lifted, its sensitive nostrils quivering, its reddish-brown coat a tawny glow against the green of the slopes behind it. Then, with a bound, it went leaping over the ground, leaving them blinking at each other and wondering whether they had really seen it.

The excitement at seeing the graceful wild animal kept Beth and Geordie with Dougal, and the three of them surged ahead talking about it. Alone with Alan, Deirdre felt him dragging; he was tired, and it was time for him to be given a ride on his father's back. She looked down at him. He was singing happily to himself, obviously contented to be with her, and again she was disturbed as she recalled Dougal's remark that he had not found anyone he could ask to be stepmother to his child until this summer. *Until he had met her.*

It couldn't be! She was married to Rory. A great longing for Rory swept over her. She wanted to be with him, to feel his arms around her, to hear his husky voice mocking her. It didn't matter that he wasn't in love with her, she just wanted him. Intent on getting back to the car, she hurried along, pulling Alan with her.

There was a sudden jerk at her hand. A shrill voice cried out.

'Look! Look! Ach, Deirdre, won't you look?'

As the words penetrated she stopped, looked, and felt the shock of revulsion. A snake, about two feet long, its handsome head poised and wicked-looking, its dark tongue darting furiously hissed its warning at her.

'Daddy! Daddy!' Alan's voice shrieked, and Dougal looked back and saw her standing frozen, mesmerised by the hissing snake. He came striding back.

'What is it?' she gasped.

'A male adder. He's defending his front door. See that hole in the bank there? That's probably the entrance to its den,' he replied calmly.

'It's venomous, isn't it, Uncle?' asked Geordie, coming up with Beth.

'Yes, and we're lucky to have seen it. In all the time I've been coming to the island I haven't seen such a fine specimen come out to protect its mate.'

'I'm glad you think you're lucky,' retorted Deirdre, recovering from her shock, 'I might have trodden on it if Alan hadn't shouted.'

'An eagle, a stag and now an adder. The island is honouring you with all its treasures today,' said Beth with her blithe smile.

'Or warning you about something,' murmured Dougal, and once again Deirdre heard that little bell of warning ring in her ear. Then the moment had passed, they had skirted the adder and were walking on towards the two standing stones they could see pointing towards the sky, dark and

118

primeval, eroded by the weather.

As he lingered beside the tall monoliths touching the rough, runnelled stone, Deirdre was once again beset by a longing for Rory. It was time to return to him, time to stop wandering about the island with Dougal. If she did not return to him soon he might go away and she might never see him again.

The premonition was so strong that it made her feel cold with anxiety.

'Do you think we could go back now?' she heard herself saying to Dougal. He turned and looked at her with narrowed eyes.

'Och, not yet, Deirdre. We're having a super time,' objected Geordie.

'I'm tired,' complained Alan, 'piggyback, Daddy.' He reached up his skinny little arms to his father, who obligingly squatted so that the child could climb on to his back.

'Deirdre's tired too,' said Dougal, standing up with Alan on his back. He smiled down at her. 'You want to get back to Rory, don't you?' he said.

'How did you guess?'

'A feeling I had. Hasn't it struck you that we're on the same wavelength?'

'Telepathy, you mean?' She was startled.

'Something like that. Since both of us have a touch of the Cel in us, it's possible that we're more susceptible to such psychic phenomena than others are. And then our surroundings, the quiet isolation of this island, its legacy of myths and ghosts, make one even more aware that transference of thought or feeling is possible. I might even go further, and suggest to you that the appearance in turn of the eagle, the stag and the adder were all attempts on the part of Rory to get in touch with you.'

'Oh!' she exclaimed, half-laughing to cover up her deep disturbance. 'How fantastic can you get?' she added mockingly. 'You must have been reading too many books on the subject.'

'Yes, I have, as a matter of fact. Did you know that the

Russians have gone a long way in research into spiritualistic phenomena?'

He held forth on the subject while they walked to the estate car, but she only half listened because her mind was possessed by one thought. She must get back to Rory.

When they arrived at the house she went with Alan and the twins straight into the kitchen where, as usual at that time of day, Margot was preparing high tea.

'Your grandfather came on the afternoon ferry,' she announced to the children. 'He's in the garden now talking to Kirsty and Rory. Take Deirdre to meet him. You're staying to tea, of course?' she added to Deirdre.

'Thank you. If Rory wants to.'

'He wants to. Go along now, he's been a bit restless this afternoon. Missed you, I think.' Margot's smile was knowing as if she shared a secret with Deirdre.

Deirdre followed the twins and Alan through the house, and out through the french windows which led from the dining room on to a small terrace of stone. The sight of Rory leaning back on a lounger brought a flush to her cheeks, and made her heart beat faster. If there had been no one else present she would have crept up behind him, placed a hand on his shoulder and asked him to guess who she was; but Kirsty was there, sitting on a low stool almost at his feet, facing him. Her sprained ankle seemed to be forgotten—or it possibly had never existed. In another deck chair a stockily-built, broad-shouldered man with grey hair and a grey beard was sitting, leaning forward as he talked.

As the twins crashed noisily through the open window and flung themselves on their grandfather, Kirsty looked up and saw Deirdre hesitating there. Her blue eyes widened and her brilliant tormenting smile appeared.

'Well, well, here's your errant wife, Rory, with twigs in her hair and mud all over her shoes,' she drawled.

Why was Kirsty so sour? Why did she make such unkind sarcastic comments? What had she against Rory Mallon's summer wife? The thoughts winged through Deirdre's mind as she glanced down guiltily at her shoes, and touched

120

her hair with exploring fingers to remove the few twigs caught there when she had had to bend down to avoid an overhanging branch.

Slowly she advanced, and put her hand on Rory's shoulder to let him know she was beside him. To her surprise he raised a hand to cover hers and his fingers gripped possessively. He half turned his head as if to try and see her and the dark glasses glinted wickedly in the sunlight.

'Have you got twigs in your hair?' he asked softly, so that only she could hear.

'A few,' she admitted.

'I'm glad you're back.'

A few simple words. A warm handclasp. Nothing very much, but coming as they did from this man who often preferred to taunt rather than reveal his real feelings, they meant a lot to Deirdre. They cancelled out the suspicions which plagued her, chased from her mind the premonition that he might have left her, which she had felt so strongly that afternoon. They kindled a small flame of hope in her heart which flickered then grew steady, as the flame of a newly-lit candle illuminates a place which has been dark, and makes a small golden glow amongst the shifting shadows of fear and suspicion.

They cast a spell over her, so that she sat silent beside Rory at the meal table and later on the couch in the sitting room; hearing the others talking but not actually listening to them, regarding them from her new and voluntary bondage to him with an expression of indulgent pity. They were all trying so hard to impress him in some way, to entertain him, as if they sensed he was an unwilling but much-wanted guest in that house and they didn't want him to leave.

'By the way,' Ian Fairlie's crisp business executive's voice seemed to slice through the haze of her spell, 'I ran into Bob Carmichael the other day. They're back from the Far East and are coming over to see us. They want to see Alan, of course.'

'I wondered if they'd arrived. When Megan last wrote to

me she said they hoped to come.' Margot turned to Deirdre and added, 'They're Alan's other grandparents, Sorcha's people. Bob is in the Diplomatic Service and they've been in Singapore for a few years. Wasn't he interested in mountaineering at one time, Ian?'

'Interested? That's an understatement,' scoffed Dougal. 'He led an expedition to Anapurna. About fifteen years ago, wasn't it, Dad? Perhaps you know something about it, Rory?'

'Not much.' Rory's answer was cool, noncommittal, and Deirdre glanced at him. Below the dark glances she read the usual signs of strain on his face; a tautening of his mouth, a flaring of his nostrils. She could feel impatience throbbing through him as his thigh pressed against hers. She slipped her hand down casually between them, and his hand came down on it and gripped tightly. He was glad she was there with him, and as she felt desire flicker Deirdre smiled to herself, although she did not know it, a slight mysterious smile.

Looking up, she encountered Kirty's bright blue stare. 'Poor Kirsty,' she thought, from the safety of that new world which she shared with Rory, 'she doesn't know what it's like to be wanted. For all her beauty she has never known what I have known and will know this summer. She hasn't had what is richest and best.'

Her glance moved on and met the dark brown sadness of Dougal's eyes, seeing him as a shy reserved man haunted by his failure to hold and keep one wife, and so reluctant to take another.

'Let's go home.' Rory's voice was a husky whisper in her ear and the candle glow in her heart seemed to widen and burn more strongly. Home. He thought of the cottage as home; where he wanted to be at this moment with her.

There was an attempt to detain them longer, but with his usual ruthless determination Rory blocked it, and soon they were out on the road swinging along hand in hand in the twilight.

Above the curve of the moors the western sky was pale

green sprinkled with the faint glitter of stars. Away to their right the sea gleamed with a silvery sheen beneath the encroaching indigo shadows of night creeping across it from the east, and the moon was a crescent of pale gold. Down by the tranquil bay the walls of the cottage glinted white amongst the clustering bushes.

'We're nearly there,' said Deirdre softly.

'I wished we'd never left,' replied Rory with a vehemence which surprised her. 'I wish I'd stayed there and not gone to Darroch House this afternoon. The effort of being polite of not saying what I think was almost too much for me—if you hadn't returned when you did I don't know what I might have done.'

Deirdre was startled.

'Oh, why? Didn't you have a pleasant time with Margot?'

'Margot was all right,' he muttered, 'it was that little

'That isn't a nice way to talk about anyone,' she remonstrated.

'Can you think of any other way to describe her?' he countered savagely. 'And what did she mean by calling you my "errant wife". What the hell was she getting at?'

'I think she must have meant that I'd wandered away from you for the afternoon,' she replied quietly. A thought occurred to her. Was it possible that he resented her outings with Dougal and the children—particularly this afternoon's outing when Kirsty had not been with them?

'Do you object to me exploring the island without you?' she asked cautiously. Rory frowned.

'No. Why should I? I'm glad you feel that you don't have to stay with me all the time. Freedom of action is something I value very highly for myself, so I can hardly deny it to others. Besides. . . .' he hesitated, then said more slowly, 'when I'm able to see I shan't stay with you all the time, and I hope you won't expect me to, Deirdre. I hope you're not the clinging type.'

'I hope I'm not, too,' she replied lightly, trying to cover up the pain his words caused. 'What else did Kirsty say?'

'Nothing honest and outright, it was all hints and suggestions. She must have been born with a wasp's sting for a tongue.'

Deirdre giggled suddenly.

'What's funny?' he demanded, coming to a halt and swinging her round to face him. Breast to breast they stood on the shadowed road; behind him she could see the green light had gone from the sky, and the stars now sparkled with frosty brilliance.

'How can a bitch have a wasp's sting?' she retorted, and laughed.

'You know damn well what I mean,' he growled, pulling her into his arms. His cheek against hers, he added, 'I love it when you laugh. I wish. . . .' He broke off and his mouth found hers. He had kissed her with passion before, but this was passion with a difference; passion underlined with desperation, as if time were running out and this was the last opportunity for him to find what he was seeking.

And it was to that desperation she responded in a way she had been unable to respond before—easily, naturally, holding him closely, glad to be there. But strong as she was, she felt faint and giddy when he stood away from her and she had to hold on to him.

'Why are we wasting time out here?' he murmured.

'I . . . I don't know. It was your idea. You stopped,' she countered rather weakly.

One arm around her, he urged her forward down the hill so that they were almost running, and gravel crunched under their feet as they went up to the cottage door. Rory opened it, finding the knob presumably by instinct, and then they were in the peat-scented darkness of the little hallway. In the bedroom moonlight shed a faint radiance on the bed, striping it with nuptial white and striking golden sparks from the brass rails.

This time there was no attempt on her part to escape. There was no holding back. The hours she had spent away from him during the past days had shocked her into the realisation that if she didn't take all he offered, she might

124

spend her days regretting that she had held back. At last she was fully awake from her long slumber, and when he murmured triumphantly, 'I told you it wouldn't always be against your will,' she could do nothing but agree with him.

CHAPTER EIGHT

THE weather continued fine. Soft airs blew over the island. Heather bloomed in purple profusion on the brown moors, vying with the yellow blaze of whin bushes. Grain growing in the crofter's fields took on harvest colours, a patchwork of bronze and ochre amongst the meadows and in the small garden of the cottage delicate purple and pink fuchsia bells swung amongst dark green leaves that clustered against the old grey dry-stone walls, where huge hydrangea blossoms, blue and pink, turned their round faces to the sun.

Against the azure skies the three mountains lifted their aloof curves—the highest, Beinn an Oir, living up to its name as its quartzite-crowned summit glinted gold in the sunshine.

The days passed slowly, each one having a breath-holding, tiptoeing quality for Deirdre. She took them as they came, looking neither backward nor forward, enjoying the fragile happiness they offered to the full and keeping at bay the fear that it could not last. But sometimes at night she would lie awake long after Rory had gone to sleep and listen to the sad singing of the seals, wondering if the next day would match the one she had just known. For although they were lovers, he had not said he loved her.

She did not stay with him all the time; with the twins, Dougal and Alan she discovered more of the island, visiting the little burial place at Earnadail where it was said the early Christian saint St Ernan had been buried. She called on Mrs Buie, who lived in one of the old stone crofting houses with a thatched roof, and watched her milk her glossy coated Highland cows by hand; she traced the burn to its source half way up a mountainside and learned to fish in it, actually catching a trout. Although Rory was always invited to go on these outings he never went with them, preferring to stay alone at the cottage. But when she returned he seemed glad to have her back, and would listen attentively to her accounts of her activities.

One afternoon when she returned, however, she found him cool and unresponsive, and as she watched the blue of the sky slowly disappear as oyster-coloured clouds spread across it, she felt her spirits slowly sink downwards. It looked very much as if the golden days were coming to an end.

This feeling was increased the next morning, as she sat at the desk and stared out at the misty greyness.

'I think it's going to rain,' she said sadly. 'The sky's like lead, and visibility is poor.'

'Most good things come to an end some time,' replied Rory curtly.

She turned round from the deak and looked at him. His withdrawal of the previous evening had developed into a brittleness of mood which made him difficult to please; several times they had come close to having a yelling match. She had decided that his irritability was due to the fact that they were in the middle of describing the day that he and his friend Euan had roped together to reconnoitre that sheer face of rock from which they had fallen.

Once again he was having to live through the ordeal; the long wait, watching his friend die, feeling himself freeze and lose his sight, and it was all taxing his nerves.

But his words about all good things having to come to an end sounded like a knell of doom to Deirdre. They had been on the island almost four weeks, during which time a new way of life had opened up for her as she had adjusted to being his wife. Now it was nearly the end of August.

126

Summer was passing, and with its passing there was the grim possibility of this new life of hers coming to an end when she had just begun to appreciate it. Dread lay heavy within her.

'Deirdre, sleep beauty, wake up,' he teased gently, grasping a length of her hair and pulling it.

'Rory . . . I must tell you . . .' she said jerkily, 'I'm not beautiful.'

Surprise held him silent for a moment. Then his mouth twisted impatiently, as if he couldn't be bothered with feminine vagaries this morning.

'So what?' he drawled carelessly. 'I think I've told you before that you have enough beauty to satisfy a blind man.'

She sat stiff and silent trying to cope with that knife-thrust. *Enough to satisfy a blind man.* Didn't that mean he wouldn't be satisfied to have her as his wife when he could see her?

'Don't tell me I've won an argument so easily,' he jibed, reacting to her silence.

'I meant my face and figure. All the other women you've known have been so perfect,' she mumbled, 'I can't compete with any of them.'

'All what women?' Now he sounded amused. 'I know my hair has a touch of red in it, but believe me, that's the only resemblance I have to Casanova. I've never collected women as he did.'

'I was thinking of the women you used to photograph . . . Louise Bolton, for instance,' she said tentatively.

'That was purely a business relationship. Anyway, she was skinny and sharp, like an icicle.'

'Then there's Toni,' she suggested, and when there was no response she added quickly, 'and Kirsty.'

'Kirsty!' Astonishment crackled in his voice. 'What makes you think I've ever had anything to do with her, apart from having to put up with her bitchy remarks?'

'She told me she could have attracted you five years ago, if it hadn't been for Sorcha,' Deirdre said in a small voice.

'She told you that?' Rory was incredulous. 'Sheer fantasy on her part. The lengths some women will go to never fails to amaze me! I scarcely noticed her.' He paused, looking suddenly worried. 'Perhaps if I had, she wouldn't be trying to cause troubles now.'

'How is she trying to cause trouble?' she asked.

He paced away from her so she could only see his back, and his hand fidgeted with one of the knobs of the brass bed end.

'By the things she says,' he muttered. 'She was here yesterday, saying them. I told her to clear out and not come back.'

'What did she say? Was it about Sorcha?'

'No, not about her.' He shrugged his shoulders. 'It doesn't matter—could be I was feeling hypersensitive. Now, where were we up to? We'll not get this finished if we don't get a move on.'

Turning back to the typewriter with a sigh, she realised that once again he had evaded her questioning. He avoided the subject of Toni, and the only reason she could think of was that Toni was too close to him.

A few minutes later her attention was caught by a flash of red beyond the dry stone wall; the post van. With a word of explanation to Rory, she went out to the porch to take the letter from the cheery postman who greeted her in his sing-song Hebridean voice.

Returning slowly to the bedroom, Deirdre read the typewritten words on the long envelope. It was for Rory, and was postmarked London.

'For you,' she said, and he nodded.

'It'll be from Dick, I've been expecting it. Thought he would have written before this.'

'It's been a while coming. Maybe he didn't address it correctly,' she said.

'Open it and read it,' he ordered impatiently.

In the envelope she found a single sheet of paper, and another envelope which was sealed and obviously contained a letter. She took out the single sheet and read the letter. Dick hoped they were having a good holiday; he and two friends, Bernie and Tom, would be setting off for Scotland the next day and would be arriving—

'Today!' gasped Deirdre, making rapid calculations. 'They'll be here today. He says they'll stay for one night only, and catch the ferry back tomorrow and drive up to Fort William.'

'They're going to climb Ben Nevis,' said Rory. 'Good. They're coming just in time. Does he say anything else?'

'Only that everything seemed all right at your studio and that he found the enclosed letter there. It had been pushed under the door, not posted. He thought the bills could wait until you return.' Deirdre folded up the letter. 'Why do you say they're coming just in time?'

'In time for a celebration,' he replied with a grin.

Her heart leapt in her throat, making speech difficult for a few seconds. What did he mean? What was there to celebrate? The return of his sight?

'Why should there be a celebration?' she managed to say at last.

'Does there have to be a reason?' he countered. 'I like parties, and the arrival of friends is sufficient reason for me to celebrate. We'll go out to dinner at the hotel in Craighouse. Margot was telling me they provide a good meal there.'

She stared at him in perplexity. This was the first time he had wanted to go out and eat in public since he had lost his sight, and she couldn't help feeling that there was more to it than just a desire to have a party with his friends.

'Who is the other letter from?' he asked.

'I haven't taken it out yet.' She delved into the long envelope and took out the other, thicker envelope. The feel of it was familiar and the sight of the elegant sloping writing, so expressive of Toni's elegant physical appearance, seemed to make her blood freeze.

'Come on, hurry up, love. Who's it from?' demanded Rory impatiently.

She slit the envelope open and pulled out the single sheet of paper. Her eyes went quickly over the message written there, and she felt colder than ever.

'It's . . . it's from Toni,' she said in strangled tones.

'Oh?' he seemed taken aback, and his eyebrows slanted frowningly above the dark glasses. 'A belated message of congratulations, I suppose,' he said and his voice rasped queerly.

'Yes,' she whispered, 'a message of congratulations.'

It was the first time she had ever lied, and it worked; he didn't ask her to read the letter aloud, so she replaced it in its envelope and laid it on the desk. But the few sentences Toni had written in her casual way seemed to be printed on her mind. They danced before her eyes all morning as she listened to Rory telling her, in terse phrases which seemed to be torn out of him, all that had happened on the mountainside in far-away Kumoa earlier in the year.

So much for holding her breath and walking tiptoe through the last few days, afraid in case she shattered the golden idyll she had created for herself. With a few careless words Toni had shattered it. And now, added to the pain inflicted by the letter, she had this awful feeling of guilt because she had lied about it to Rory.

'Deirdre.' His voice was sharp. 'You're not listening. What the hell's the matter with you this morning?'

She could have countered by asking him what the hell was the matter with him. Why was he so bad-tempered this morning? Why had he been so cool and withdrawn last night? Why hadn't he made love to her?

She caught her breath, her hand to her mouth. She mustn't think like that. It showed a weakness. It showed how much he had taken over.

'I don't know,' she quavered. 'I don't seem able to concentrate. I have a headache and I feel a bit sick.' Both were true.

'You seemed all right when you got up this morning,' he challenged. 'Your sickness seems to have developed very quickly.'

'I know, but . . .'

'You're a poor liar, Deirdre, it's your puritan upbring-

130

ing,' he scoffed. 'It's the letter from Toni—it's upset you for some reason. Come on, tell me, what does she want you to do this time?'

He sounded indulgently amused, that was all, and she realised she hadn't told him that the letter had been addressed to him only.

'She isn't married after all,' she began stiltedly, and saw him stiffen. 'The American wasn't what he had seemed. He walked out on her, so she returned to London the day we left.' Deirdre gulped, conscious of hysteria rising within her, she wanted to laugh wildly. 'She called on you the next day. If you'd waited twenty-four hours you wouldn't have had to marry me and I needn't have come here. I could have gone to Spain instead.'

He turned away, and she found herself remembering the way he had once averted his face in hospital because he had been disappointed that she had visited him and not Toni.

'Oh, I can't stand it!' she exclaimed suddenly, and sprang up from the chair and ran from the room. She grabbed her anorak from the hook in the hall and stepped into the porch, throwing off her slippers and stepping into her wellington boots automatically, because she had learned the hard way not to go walking without wearing them on this island. She thought she heard Rory coming out of the bedroom, thought she heard him call,

'Wait, Deirdre——'

But, as once before, she didn't wait. She fled through the porch door, closing it behind her with a bang. Along the silvery beach she sped, floundering as she went, blind and deaf to the sea's sullen surge and the cries of the sea-birds, not interested today in any shells which might be hidden in the long ribbons of seaweed. Intent only to be as far as possible from Rory, because she could not bear to see him suffer.

She stopped running only when she had no more breath. Panting, she trudged by the edge of the water, her head down and her hands in her pockets, going in the direction of the headland where the tall haunted house stood, dark and forbidding. She didn't notice when a wave of the incoming tide slopped over her foot, so sunk was she in the depths of an unhappiness she had never thought it possible to experince. The depths of despair.

She did not realise that someone was coming along the beach towards her, and was surprised when a voice hailed her. Looking up, she saw Dougal and the twins, with Alan dawdling behind them.

'We're just coming to ask you if you'd like to go fishing with us in the bay,' said Geordie.

'The bay?' she repeated woodenly, forcing herself to appear normal. She knew that Dougal's dark eyes missed very few details.

'Yes, our bay,' said Beth, 'the Bay of the Young Woman it's called in Gaelic, only I can't speak the language.'

'Will you come?' persisted Geordie.

Deirdre looked at Dougal. As she had expected he was watching her closely, a deep concern in his brown eyes.

'Shall I?' she asked him.

'We would be glad to have your company, Deirdre, you know that,' he replied gravely, 'but I'd better tell you what's involved. We go out in the bigger of our two boats, anchor it and put our lines over the side and wait for bites. It's an ideal day for it; the sea calm, the sky overcast.'

'We should get some big'uns,' said Geordie enthusiastically. 'Come with us and see if you can catch a cod.'

She glanced back at the cottage. Rory had not followed her, but then he didn't follow, he led, she thought mournfully.

'I'd like to come,' she said simply, and turned to walk with them along the beach and round the foot of the headland to the Bay of the Young Woman.

From the boathouse they dragged the big sturdy open boat down the slip into the grey water; water as grey as Rory's eyes, which he had kept covered with the dark glasses for a long time now during the daytime—and when the lights were on in the evening so that she hadn't seen them, Deirdre realised with a little jolt of surprise. He took

132

the glasses off only after the lights were out, and put them on as soon as he woke up in the morning.

A few pulls on the outboard engine and it sputtered into life, and soon the boot was moving out into the bay. From the water the house looked gaunt, high-shouldered and mysterious and the cliffs down which the young woman was supposed to have fallen, shrieking to her death loomed dourly over the water like a threat.

'The tide must have been in,' Deirdre murmured, and Dougal replied at once,

'It was, and she couldn't swim. I imagine it was easy to accomplish on a wild dark night.'

She glanced at him. He was sitting in the stern of the boat steering, his back to the house, and since she was in the bow she was facing him. On the thwart between them sat the three children.

Once again he had picked up her thoughts, had known instinctively what she was talking about. As Kirsty had once pointed out, she had much in common with him, more than she had with Rory; a similar upbringing and background, education producing similar attitudes and similar interests.

They approached the entrance to the bay and anchored the boat there, just on the edge of its smooth sheltered water. The fishing lines were produced, and with wicked-looking hooks attached to them were put over the side. Then they all sat still, occasionally moving the lines up and down so that the bright hooks would flash in the darkness of the deep and attract the fish.

Apart from the slapping of water against the side of the boat and the occasional screech of a sea-bird it was quiet. The sea stretched emptily away to the distant coast of Kintyre, which was blurred with mist, and within the bay the water shone with an eerie white light. Beyond its curving shore the moors crowded darkly. No colour today, no blaze of heather or glow of whin, just perpetual sodden greyness.

'Tomorrow we might go to Port Ellen, on Islay,' said

Beth suddenly, unable to stay quiet for long.

'I remember singing a song about Islay when I was at school,' said Deirdre. 'It began like this: "Westering home and a song in the air." I'm afraid I can't remember any more.'

' "Light in the eye and it's goodbye to care,
    Laughter of love and a welcoming there,
    Isle of my heart, my own one." '

Beth finished the verse in a soft sweet soprano.

'It's a lovely island,' she added, 'very green and soft.'

'But it's not as good as this island,' said Geordie, with fierce loyalty. 'You can't have as much fun on it as you can here. It isn't as wild and empty. I think like Mum does, this is our "dear" island.'

'Now that I've seen more of it I know what you mean,' said Deirdre. 'But I'd have liked to have seen some more islands before I leave this part of the world.'

'Leave? When are you leaving?' The twins spoke in unison as they often did, their voices loud with surprise so that Dougal turned to say irritably,

'How do you two expect us to catch anything, when you can't keep quiet or sit still? Every fish must have been frightened away by now.'

'Sorry, Uncle, but Deirdre says she's going to leave,' said Beth.

'Are you?' he asked, and over the twins' dark heads his eyes asked questions.

It had slipped out unwittingly, because her mind had been on the subject of leaving; of Rory leaving her, or possibly of her leaving Rory. She could not be sure which way round it would eventually be now that Toni was back in the picture, free and waiting in London, but she was convinced it would happen.

'I don't know when; soon, I think,' she answered Dougal.

'But Rory said you'd be here until the middle of September, if not longer,' complained Beth. 'Geordie and I hoped you'd be her when Mum and Dad come for us in their boat. They should be here soon. Dad says he wants to go through Corryvreckan.'

'What's that?' asked Deirdre, seeing a way to divert the conversation from the subject of leaving.

'It's a whirlpool between this island and Scarba. You can only go through it in a small boat when the weather is calm and the tide is right,' said Dougal. 'Corrie means pothole or boiler, and that's what the water does in rough weather; it swirls and bubbles as if it's boiling, making it impassable. And Vreckan is taken from the tartan rock which stands on the shore near it.'

'And of course there are many tales told about it,' said Deirdre with a smile.

'Of course,' he said, smiling back. 'It's been called the lair of some great sea beast, belonging to the all-powerful sea gods. Some people have thought that it's actually the entrance to the country of the gods below the sea. My favourite tale is the one which calls it Old Woman Winter's wash pot. There she boils her blankets and sheets on a night of winter storm, and the next day you can see them spread out white on the tops of mountains, or after an extra big wash over the lower land as well.'

'As snow,' whispered Deirdre, delighted by the idea. 'That will be my favourite story too.'

There were other stories told about the islands that afternoon, and Deirdre sat entranced listening to them. She would never forget these four people who had shown her their 'dear' island. In particular she would never forget Dougal; the quiet, deeply sensitive man, touched by tragedy, still mourning for the wife who had left him because she could not help herself.

And having known Rory and felt the pull of that strange magnetism which she was sure he didn't know he possessed, she could understand the sad wraith called Sorcha, who once she had laid eyes on him had forgotten Dougal and the fey little boy, who even now leaned against her and whispered,

'I don't want you to leave, Deirdre . . . ever. I want you to be my mummy.'

The sudden silence was shocking. The twins looked embarrassed. They were old enough to understand the implication of such a suggestion, and their dark eyes flickered uneasily from Dougal to Deirdre and back again.

Dougal's weatherbeaten face had lost some colour and his eyes had gone black, but he spoke to the child gently as usual.

'You know that can't be, Alan. Deirdre belongs to Rory.'

Belongs to Rory. She knew he was explaining in simple words so that the child would understand, but how well he had described her situation! At one time she would have stated with fierce independence that she belonged to no one but herself, and that she would never belong to anyone else. But now the idea that she belonged to Rory did not rouse one little spark of resentment, because she knew it was true—even though she had to accept that Rory did not belong to her.

'He could leave her there with us when he goes away,' said Alan obstinately. 'Then she could be my mummy.'

'It's not quite as easy as that,' said Deirdre. 'Much as I like you, Alan, I couldn't stay with you. I have to stay with Rory, to look after him while he's blind. I promised him I would stay with him.'

Her voice wobbled a little and she had to break off, turning away to look at the water. At that moment Geordie gave a shout.

'A bite, a bite!' he cried exultantly, and began to haul in his line. The excitement of landing the silver quivering fish made them forget the awkward moment, and from then on they were all too intent on catching more fish to talk about anything else.

An hour later they returned triumphantly to the shore. The twins raced off up the path to the house, with Alan trailing behind them, to show off their catch to their grandparents. Deirdre lingered with Dougal to help him tie up the boat to the small stone jetty.

'Coming up for a cup of tea?' he asked her when the boat had been made fast.

'No, thank you, I'd better go back to the cottage, I didn't tell Rory I was going out, he'll be wondering where I am.'

'You answered Alan very well,' he said, his eyes down as they watched his hands coiling a rope. 'You answered a question I've been wanting to ask for myself many times these past few days.'

Absorbing the implication which lay behind his words, she decided it would be wise for her not to say anything.

'What happens when Rory's sight returns, Deirdre? Do you have to stay with him then?' he probed carefully.

The question disturbed her and brought to mind the other promise she and Rory had made to each other.

'If he wants me to, yes, I will,' she said.

'And if he doesn't?' he looked up as he spoke, his eyes narrowed to watch her reaction.

Her lips felt dry and she licked them nervously, tasting salt on them from the spray churned up by the boat. She clenched her hands in the pockets of her jacket, trying to annul the pain caused by being brought face to face with a reality she had been trying to avoid.

'I'll have to cross that bridge when I come to it,' she replied steadily.

'I suppose so. I'd like you to know I'll be interested in the outcome,' he said, showing more self-confidence than she had ever seen in him before. 'I know a widower with a small boy is not an attractive bargain to any woman these days, when there are so many alternatives, but as you've noticed, Alan does require the stability and affection a woman like yourself could bring to him. He needs *you*, Deirdre.'

She was conscious of irritation. Was that to be her life, being needed by people who wanted help? Was she never to be loved for what she was, and not just for what she could bring?

'I agree with you that he needs someone,' she said quietly, 'but I'm necessarily the ideal substitute for Sorcha. You still believe Rory stole her from you, don't you?'

'I have to put the blame on him. If I don't, I'm faced

with the possibility that she never really loved me and married me only because I came along at the right time in her life to shield her from her difficulties.'

He spoke harshly, and his dark gaze flicked away from hers up to the house as if he didn't wish to face the accusation which might appear in her expression.

'Which you did,' she murmured.

'Which I did,' he repeated, the melancholy look back on his face. 'But the shield I offered wasn't strong enough.'

'But do you think it's fair to blame him when he isn't guilty, when he did nothing?' she exclaimed.

Dougal shrugged. 'He can take it. He's one of those strong characters who can take blame without buckling under it.'

'Oh, Dougal, wouldn't it be better to put it all behind you? I don't say you should forget Sorcha, but you should stop letting her haunt you, as the young woman who was drowned here haunted her husband. You did your best for her.' She put her hand on his arm urgently.

'I suppose you're right,' he muttered, placing his hand over hers. 'Perhaps I shouldn't come here where it all happened. The trouble is that I love this place, and I can't imagine taking my holidays anywhere else.'

'If you married again you would cease to be haunted.'

'Only if I married the right person, and that seems to be impossible too. Rory has all the luck,' he said bitterly.

'You mustn't say that.' She tried to remove her hand, but he held it tightly.

'Why shouldn't I, it's true. He has you. You're a very lovely person, Deirdre, in many ways.' There was a strange glow in his eyes. Then he did an odd thing, odd, that is, for one of his race. He lifted her hand and kissed the back of it. 'There, that's the only homage I dare pay to you while you're Rory's wife.'

'And even that is too much,' she retorted in a low voice, snatching her hand away. She was suddenly afraid of him. 'I must go.'

'Yes, you must go back to him, to cook his supper and

make him comfortable,' he said with a sigh. 'I wonder if he realises how lucky he is.'

'Goodbye, Dougal,' she said firmly, and turned on her heel to walk along the narrow rim of beach which curved under the looming cliffs of the headland. She had difficulty in getting round to the other bay because the tide was still high, and at one point it covered the narrow rim of sand and forced her to climb over the rocks. Several times she slipped on wet seaweed and fell to her knees, banging them on the hard stones and ripping her pants.

But at last she was over them and racing along the beach back to the white cottage, returning as fast as she had left it. She longed to be with Rory again, not caring any more whether he still loved Toni, just wanting to be with him.

Reaching the house, she twisted open the door and flung herself into the porch, kicked off her wellingtons and went into the kitchen. Rory wasn't there and the fire was out, for the first time since they had arrived. She scurried into the bedroom; he wasn't there either. He had gone out.

The panic Deirdre had felt once before when he had gone walking alone rose sickeningly within her. Hand to her throat to try and still the tumultuous beating of the puse there, she told herself not to be silly, that he was quite capable of walking out on his own. She didn't have to be with him all the time to guide him and watch every step he took, and he wouldn't like it if she did.

Then she noticed the envelope on the floor and picked it up. It was the one which had contained the letter from Toni, and it was empty.

Deirdre frowned in puzzlement. She was sure she had put the letter back in the envelope. Who could have taken it out? Where was it?

Hastily she looked through the papers scattered about on the desk. It wasn't there. The waste paper basket caught her attention; yes, it was there, screwed up into a ball flung there by an angry hand. By Rory's hand?

But he wouldn't have been able to find the letter, let alone read it, then screw it up and hurl it accurately into the basket. Rory couldn't see. Or could he?

The thought set her heart beating wildly again. She had suspected it several times but had never had the courage to ask him, and even now her mind shied away from facing up to the reason why she didn't want to ask him. The specialist had said it might come back suddenly once Rory had fully recovered from his ordeal on the mountain, and there was no doubt in her mind that he had been back to full strength for a while.

She stood for a minute, staring out at the rain which had been threatening all day and was now drifting down in hazy drizzle, and slowly she came to a conclusion. She could no longer put off asking Rory. She had to find him; ask him if he could see and take the consequences.

CHAPTER NINE

PUSHED by a sense of urgency, Deirdre ran out into the porch again, stepped into her boots and hurried out of the door into the wet clinging drizzle. Since she hadn't met Rory on her way back from the headland, she assumed that he had walked to their favourite place where the burn foamed into the sea, so she turned in that direction.

The damp air was full of the scents of earth and sea, of damp pine needles and rotting leaves, of washed up seaweed and salt water. As she drew near to the big boulders which marked the mouth of the burn she looked round expectantly, but no tall figure with wide shoulders under a cream sweater appeared. There was no sign of him.

For a moment she stood by the busy tinkling stream, watching the clear water slipping perpetually over smooth half-sunken rocks; seeing the dark seaweed lift and fall under the surface where a current swirled, and her thoughts swirled too.

If Rory could see, why hadn't he told her he could? If he could see, why had he asked her to read Dick's letter to him? Why had he said she had enough beauty to satisfy a blind man only that morning? Why? Why? There was only one way she could satisfy such curiosity. Find him and ask him. But where was he?

Panic returned again. Maybe he had walked up to the pool; another favourite place, but a dangerous one too. Often she had warned him not to go there by himself in case he slipped and fell into it, fearing that he might drown.

Quickly she stepped across the burn, using the stepping stones, and made her way along a path which led through a wood of dwarf trees of oak, birch and holly, to a glade beside a deep pool which was fed by a small waterfall.

Standing at the edge of the pool, she looked down at it. It was several feet deep and usually when the sunlight slanted through the branches of the trees the water was so clear that it was possible to see the stones at the bottom of it, glinting gold and purple and green, where they were covered with moss. But today, without the kindly sunlight, it looked dark and deeper than ever, full of mystery. Even as she stood still there, wondering if Rory had returned to the cottage down the path on the other side so that she had missed seeing him, Deirdre felt her foot slip on the mossy bank. How easy it would be to fall in and drown.

Pulling her thoughts back from such an uneasy track, she decided to cross the pool by the stepping stones which edged its lower rim. They were slippery, and in her hurry she lost her balance on one of them when it turned beneath her foot; for a few seconds her arms wavered wildly in the air as she tried to regain her balance, then the rock turned even more, and suddenly she was in the pool. The very thing she had been afraid might happen to Rory had happened to her!

Water poured over her head, cold and tingling. Stumbling and staggering on the slippery stones, she at last gained her footing, sloshed over to the side of the pool and waded

141

out of it.

If she hadn't felt so cold she would have laughed at her own predicament. How like her to have such an accident! She must look a mess, soaked to the skin, with her hair straggling over her shoulders like a wet black shawl.

Pushing her way through the tangle of bracken and interlacing brambles, she made her way back to the mouth of the burn with one thought uppermost, she must get back and change out of her wet clothing.

As she approached the sea she heard Rory calling to her, and her heart bounded with relief. He wasn't lost or hurt after all.

'Deirdre? Where are you? What are you doing?'

'I'm here! I'm coming!' she called back.

Then she saw him, tall and lithe, coming towards her, his sweater damp with rain and his hair wet. He was coming straight towards her, striding along without a stumble as if he could see where he was going.

She stood and waited, wondering if he would stop and listen to find out where she was. He did stop a few feet away from her, but he didn't put his head to one side as he usually did when he was listening intently, and his poised wary stillness reminded her of the stag she had seen when walking with Dougal and the twins. He looked alert, ready to bound away if danger came too close to him.

'What the hell have you been doing?' he exclaimed, and she knew then that he could see her.

She went up to him, put a hand on his arm and stared up, trying to see through the screening darkness of the glasses.

'You can see, can't you?' she whispered. 'You can see me.'

His mouth took on a sardonic curve.

'It's taken you a long time to guess, sweetheart,' he replied.

'Oh, I'm so glad!' she cried, flinging her arms round him impulsively.

For once his arms did not come around her, he remained

142

still and rather stiff in her embrace.

'I bet you are,' he said, and the irony in his voice puzzled her so that she drew back from him. 'You're soaked to the skin. What happened?'

'I fell into the pool,' she explained.

His mouth twitched and he began to laugh. Suddenly she was beating at his chest with her doubled fists.

'Oh, stop it, stop laughing! It wasn't funny. I was looking for you. I was afraid you'd tripped over something and hurt yourself. I was afraid you'd fallen in the stream, I was worried sick about you!'

'Well, you don't have to worry about me any more,' he said, grasping her arms and pushing her away from him. 'Your responsibility for a blind man is at an end. As you've guessed, I can see.'

'But where have you been?'

'When you didn't come back I went up to Darroch House to see if you'd gone there, and to remind you that we're having visitors. I'd just got there when you left, and returned by the shore. So I came back down the road and reached the cottage as you ran out of it; I yelled after you, but you didn't hear me. Then Dick and the others drove up, or I'd have come after you sooner.'

The coldness of his manner was penetrating at last. Deirdre realised, unhappily and belatedly, the significance of the return of his sight. He could see her, and the mess she was in; he could see how plain she was, how inelegant, how ordinary. He could make comparisons between her and Toni. And now he knew that Toni was free and he wasn't blind he wouldn't need her any more Nor would he want her.

She shivered, and then sneezed. She felt more miserable than she had felt when she had left him in the bedroom earlier.

'You need a hot bath and a good rub down after a soaking in cold water like that,' he said practically. 'Come on, let's get back to the cottage.'

Putting an arm about her shoulders, he urged her along

143

the path. Outside the cottage a strange car was parked beside the grey one, and when they entered the porch she heard the sound of men's voices coming from the kitchen.

She couldn't have the bath, because there wasn't any hot water because the fire had gone out, but she had the good rub down. Rory gave it to her personally, with a big bath towel. And he wasn't gentle about it, so that by the time he had finished she was gasping and pink-skinned, and he was laughing at her exclamations of protest.

He caught her against him, and for a moment of exquisite torture held her towel-sheathed glowing body hard against his; she could feel the edge of his hands digging into her waist. Desire flared with her, and she wanted to put her arms around his neck, to kiss him to show him once again she was glad he could see; to invite him to show her that nothing had changed between them, that he still wanted her even though he could see her.

But even as the feeling flashed comet-like through her, it brought in its wake a reactionary shyness which cooled the impulse before she could take action. Once again her mind took over as the knowledge that those long blue-grey eyes, now uncovered, were focussing and seeing her, made her spirit quail. She withdrew from his arms, hitching the towel up about her.

'Thank you, I'll get dressed now,' she said primly.

'Well, don't forget we're going out for dinner,' he said as he turned away towards the door. 'You might tell me where you've hidden that bottle of whisky we brought with us, and I'll make you a hot toddy.'

She told him and he went out. Alone, she searched for dry underwear, the glow from the rub down was wearing off and she sneezed several times. Once she was dressed in bra and briefs she took out the long gown made from green wool which she had seen weeks ago in the shop window in Regent Street. She had bought it on impulse, thinking that though she was marrying in haste she ought to have something by way of a trousseau, but somehow there had not seemed to be any point in wearing it when Rory hadn't been

144

able to see it.

Now she was surprised to see the difference it made to her appearance. The style of close-fitting low-cut bodice, long narrow sleeves and flaring long skirt accentuated her full breasts, made her waist seem narrower and concealed her broad hips. The green enhanced the whiteness of her fine skin, and made her eyes the same colour as the shallow sea-pools on a sunny day, clear and cool between the black fringes of her lashes.

Her drying hair was taking on a glossiness given to it by her recent immersion in the soft water of the burn, and not wanting its dampness to damage her dress she began to plait it into one thick braid.

She was standing in front of the mirror, working towards the end of the braid and wondering how she was going to overcome her shyness sufficiently to go into the kitchen and face Rory's friends, when the door opened and he came through it.

In the mirror she could see his reflection closing the door. He turned and stood still abruptly as he caught sight of her. In one hand he held a glass of amber fluid which steamed slightly, in the other another glass with slightly less liquid in it. He stared at her reflection, his eyes narrowed as they glanced over her appearance assessingly.

'I like that,' he said, coming up behind her. 'Now you look medieval—like my idea of Rapunzel. Why haven't you worn that dress before?'

Oh, this terrible, throat-constricting shyness! Would she ever get rid of it? While he had been unable to see properly she had not experienced it, but now she could not meet his reflected glance. She was as self-conscious as she had been that night at Toni's party, when he had turned his attention on her.

'Because I haven't been in the mood before,' she replied as lightly as she could, finishing her hair and tying green ribbon round the end of the long plait.

'So you have to fall into a pool of water to get into the right mood,' he scoffed as he handed her the glass which steamed slightly. 'Or has something else happened to put you in the right mood?'

This time she could not avoid his eyes, and as their glances met she felt a rush of warm blood to her cheeks like a blush of guilt. Quickly she looked away, down at the hot amber liquid in the glass.

'I found out you can see again,' she murmured, 'surely it's an occasion for celebration?'

'I suppose it is, from some points of view,' he said, and again the quiet irony in his voice puzzled her; his reaction to the return of his sight was so different from what she had expected. She had thought he would have been exultant, cock-a-hoop. But instead there was this cold, ironical detachment.

'Drink that up while it's hot,' he ordered brusquely, 'or it won't do any good.'

He took a drink from his own glass as he leaned against the desk and watched her. It was strange to have him looking after her, and it made her realise that he was as capable of looking after others as he was at looking after himself.

He didn't need her any more, that was why he was behaving in this detached way. The thought stormed through her, making her choke on the first sip of the hot whisky. As she spluttered and coughed she felt him take the glass from her and slap her back.

'Now I suppose you're going to tell me that happened because you're not used to strong drink,' he jibed. 'Here, drink some more.'

She sipped more. It sent a warming, heart-easing glow through her.

'How long have you been able to see?' she asked. Questions had to be asked now, while they were alone.

'A few days,' he replied, tipping up his glass and draining it.

'But why didn't you tell me at once?' she exclaimed. The situation was far worse than she had imagined. He had been seeing her when she had not known he could see, deceiving her.

146

'I wanted to be sure that it wasn't temporary. That it had come back to stay.' He spoke easily, then his mouth quirked mischievously. 'I wanted to find out how long it would take for you to guess I could see.'

Deirdre was rapidly recalling all the times she had guessed he could see, but had shied away from asking him if he could. Alarm, followed quickly by pain, ran through her. He must have been seeing for more than a few days.

'It was hardly kind of you not to tell me,' she objected in a low voice, hurt because he had kept her in ignorance. Somehow it showed that he had no trust in her.

'I learned early in life that to be kind to anyone else I usually have to defraud myself,' he replied enigmatically, 'so I gave up being kind years ago, and I'm not going to be kind now. You realise, I hope, that the return of my sight makes a difference to our relationship.'

His words froze her into immobility. She stood with her head bowed, holding the glass between her two hands in front of her. She felt like a prisoner waiting for the sentence of death to be pronounced.

'Yes, I realise that,' she said nervously.

'I'm glad you do, because it makes it easier for me to say what I'm going to say. I've decided to go to Ben Nevis with Dick and the others tomorrow.'

'Ben Nevis?' She was surprised into looking up. Blue-grey eyes, watchful between narrowed lids, met hers. 'You want to climb again? Oh, Rory, do you think you should?' She was confused. She had been so sure he had been going to say their brief marriage was over, that he wanted his freedom to go back to Toni. 'You might fall again,' she faltered.

'I might,' he agreed with a touch of grimness, 'but what concerns me is not that; I'm afraid I might not have enough nerve to rope up and climb a rock face again. I have to go with them and find out. The chance is too good for me to miss now that I'm sure I'm seeing properly.' He paused and rubbed a hand thoughtfully up and down his cheek. 'What will you do?'

She was disconcerted. Disappointment at not being invited to go with him was like a blast of cold wind, which blew out the little flame of hope she had been nursing carefully for the past few days.

'I . . . I'm not sure. Will you be taking the car?'

'I'll have to, there isn't room in Dick's car for my equipment. In fact they're a bit cramped in it, so Tom will come with me. If you need anything from the village I daresay the Fairlies would give you a lift in—or if you decided to go south they'd take you to the ferry.'

'Won't you be coming back here, then?' she quavered.

'Yes. Next week, I expect. The book still has to be finished.' He was watching her; waiting, she was sure, for some reaction. But what? Deirdre had the feeling he had been planning this for days just as he had planned their hasty marriage. He was going away and by doing so he was asserting his independence, at the same time giving her a chance to assert hers. *If you decide to go south.* He expected her to go, to be gone when he returned next week. For a few weeks she had been useful to him, but now she was an embarrassment and he wanted to be rid of her. His egotism was appalling and Elise had been right, Dick Hunter had been right. She had been out of her mind to marry him.

Either that, or hopelessly and irrevocably in love with him!

The thought jolted her out of her confusion. Anger was cold and tingling as the water of the pool had been; it cleared her mind, made her see how gullible she had been, how easily deceived. She drew herself up to her full height and looked him in the eyes; long, narrow blue-grey eyes which lent his face that touch of wildness.

'What if I've gone south before you return?' she asked. 'What will you do then?'

He didn't flinch. His eyes didn't waver. Nerves of steel, she thought with a touch of hysteria.

'I expect I'll survive,' he replied coolly, and turned to pick up his glass from the desk. 'Come and see the others as

148

soon as you're ready. Dick's been asking for you.'

He went from the room and she stood alone, clenching and unclenching her hands. She still couldn't believe it had happened after the happiness of those few golden days, when, it seemed to her, they had made such progress in their relationship; when she was sure he had been just as happy as she had. Was it to end like this?

In a numbed daze she went into the kitchen to greet Dick, and be introduced to Bernie and Tom. Talking and smiling mechanically, she suggested how they could arrange to sleep in the kitchen for the night. They all seemed delighted that Rory could see, and found nothing strange in his decision to go with them to Ben Nevis; nor did they seem to find it strange that she wasn't to accompany him. After all, they were all married and had all left their wives behind. It wasn't unusual.

They went in the two cars to the hotel, a tall white building which had once been a distillery but which had been comfortably converted into the island's only inn; and in spite of a certain coolness between herself and Rory it was a gay meal, because they were all really glad that he could see again. As it progressed the high spirits which she had expected him to show on the return of his sight came to the fore, and as a result there was a lot of laughter which drew the attention of other diners in the room, most of them holidaymakers who were staying in the hotel.

In particular Deirdre noticed a short fair man who was sitting at a table with a thin, rather nervous-looking woman whom she guessed was his wife. The man kept glancing at her and at Rory, who was sitting opposite to her his back to the room. When the man and his companion stood up to leave the dining room Dick, who was sitting next to Deirdre, said quietly,

'Don't all look at once, but there's a chap just about to go out who looks very familiar to me. I can't think of his name, though.'

Bernie glanced sideways and recognition flashed across his face.

'It's Carmichael, Bob Carmichael. He led an expedition to Anapurna once. Do you think he's staying here? Perhaps we ought to go and make ourselves known to him. He might be interested in our efforts to date.'

'Good idea,' said Tom. 'How about it, Rory?'

'You go and talk to him, if you want to, and take Dick. Deirdre and I'll go back to the cottage. I'd like to get my stuff packed ready for tomorrow.'

'All right,' said Bernie, 'come on, Tom. 'Scuse us, Deirdre.'

They went off to follow the man and his wife. Dick stayed seated, looking at Rory with an expression of quizzical puzzlement on his broad, good-humoured face.

'Why haven't you gone to worship at the feet of the hero, Dick?' asked Rory rather scornfully.

'I was going to ask you the same,' replied Dick. 'He's been looking across at you all through the meal. He knows you.'

'And I know him,' said Rory softly.

'It's not like you to hold a grudge against anyone. If you know him, why didn't you go with the other two to speak to him?' asked Dick.

'If he knows me why didn't he come over here and speak to me?' countered Rory. 'I've no grudge against him, I just don't want to put myself in a position where I might be snubbed in public.'

'But why. . . .' Dick broke off, frowned and continued, 'They're coming back, looking thoroughly put out.'

'I'm not surprised,' drawled Rory. 'Carmichael has a way of dealing with people who don't quite measure up to his personal standards of behaviour which they don't forget easily.'

Bernie and Tom both looked a little red in the face.

'He and his wife have retired to their room,' explained Bernie, 'they don't want to be disturbed. Well, know we know what he's like. Are we going back now? Shall we take some beer with us?'

As she drove back to the cottage in the fast-gathering

darkness, Deirdre was unable to ask Rory the questions which were surging up in her mind about Bob Carmichael, who was Sorcha's father, because Dick was with them. So she was glad when he asked casually,

'What exactly did you do to Carmichael which would make him want to snub you, Rory?'

'I asked him if I could go on his expedition fifteen years ago,' replied Rory drily.

'Good lord,' exclaimed Dick, 'that must have taken a bit of nerve. He turned you down, I suppose?'

'You suppose right. Not surprising really, when you think about it. I was nineteen, had no money, very little experience and had a reputation for using unconventional methods when climbing. I wasn't at all the sort of person Carmichael would consider in any way for anything,' Rory's voice was slightly bitter. 'All I had was nerve. Deirdre, don't you think you're going too fast for the state of this road?'

'I'm sorry, I was thinking of something else,' she replied. It was the first time he had ever criticised her driving, and she felt it was the measure of how he was feeling about her. It was a wonder he had allowed her to drive now he could see.

'Just like my wife,' said Dick with a laugh as if he sensed a coolness. 'Her mind wanders when she's driving, and the car wanders too, all over the road.'

With the change of subject Rory's unpopularity with Bob Carmichael was forgotten and Deirdre found she had no chance to ask the question which was bothering her most. When Rory had asked Carmichael if he could go on the expedition, had he met Sorcha then? Was it possible that been his first? If they had met previously wouldn't that his meeting with her on the island five years ago had not account for Sorcha's interest in him when he turned up again.

Even when they returned to the cottage there was no opportunity to ask the question, because they were not alone for the rest of the evening. When at last, tired and rather

151

snuffly from her immersion in the cold water of the pool, Deirdre excused herself to go to bed, Rory did not follow her into the bedroom.

For a while she lay awake in the wide bed, keyed up and waiting. She listened to the murmur of voices in the other room, willing herself to stay awake until Rory came, longing for him to come. This was their last night together in this cottage, where for a while she had known what was richest and best. Surely the time they had spent together meant something to him—or was he one of those people who could take and then forget?

But sleep crept up on her before he came, and she did not waken until she felt a hand on her shoulder and heard a familiar teasing voice saying,

'Come on, Sleeping Beauty, wake up. We're going now.'

'Going? Going where?' She sat up suddenly, rubbing sleep from her eyes, convinced it was the middle of the night until she realised sunlight was slanting through the window.

'To catch the ferry,' said Rory. 'It leaves at nine-fifty.' He looked, and sounded, coolly confident. The slate-blue sweater he was wearing under a zipped waterproof jacket emphasized the colour of his eyes and the tan of his face.

'Oh. I'd better get the breakfast,' she mumbled, pushing aside the covers. She swung her feet out of bed and stood up with her hair swirling about her shoulders, black against the pink of her befrilled long nightgown.

'Too late,' he said with a grin, 'we mountaineers are pretty good at looking after ourselves, you know. We've eaten and we've washed the dishes and put them away. Nothing for you to do this morning except laze about in the sun.'

'You should have wakened me earlier,' she protested.

'You were sleeping so soundly I hadn't the heart to disturb you. Nor last night either,' he said gently.

Their eyes met for a brief intimate moment. Then, suddenly shaky and shy, Deirdre turned away to pick up her dressing gown from the chair where she had placed it.

'I'll come and see you off, then,' she said hastily, pulling the gown on. Turning round, she found him in front of her, blocking the way. He put his hands on her shoulders.

'Are you quite sure you've nothing to tell me before I go?' he asked quietly.

Shoulders straight beneath the warm pressure of his hand, she looked at him steadily.

'No, I can't think of anything,' she said.

His eyebrows slanted in a puzzled frown.

'You're sure, Deirdre?'

'Quite sure. Have you anything to tell me?'

His hands slid over her back in a familiar caressing way as he drew her against him. Held like that she couldn't see his face unless she pulled away from him, could not tell if he were telling the truth or not when he replied.

'I've a lot to tell you,' he said softly against her hair, and then Dick shouted to him to hurry or they'd all miss the ferry. 'But there isn't time right now,' added Rory, his voice muffled.

His fingers wound in her hair to pull her head back, then his lips were warm and hard against hers. She wanted the kiss to go on; she wanted to hold him close against her until she felt the passion rising within him, making him her prisoner so that he could not go away, but another shout from Dick brought the embrace to an abrupt end.

'Listen, if you find you can't keep that promise you made, I'll understand,' said Rory gruffly. 'So long, love.'

He went from the room quickly. As she tied the belt of her dressing gown with shaky fingers and thrust her feet into her slippers she heard the roar of Dick's car starting up, and hurried outside.

Dick's car was already turning on to the road, she saw him and Bernie raise their hands to wave goodbye to her. The pale morning sunlight glinted on the sleek grey car as Rory reversed it. His hand flashed her another farewell, and then the car was gone with a low growl, to purr up the hill.

She stood for a moment, listening to the sound of the

cars retreating as they went over the hill, and wondered what Rory had meant when he said he would understand if she couldn't keep the promise she had made to him.

CHAPTER TEN

TIME spent without Rory was torture, thought Deirdre; he had gone on Tuesday, and this was only Thursday morning. He had said he would be back next week, but she had forgotten to ask which day.

It wasn't that she was afraid of being alone. It was just that after two days without him her nerves were on edge, because she could not stop her memory from behaving like a ciné film which perpetually reviewed everything they had done together since they were married. And accompanying the film was a soundtrack which had recorded some of his remarks, the more puzzling of them, and they repeated themselves over and over again in her mind until she felt she would go crazy with trying to understand them.

If you can't keep that promise you made I'll understand. And with that remark he had left her. It would have been better if he had said nothing, rather than leave her with a puzzle like that to solve.

He had been referring to the promise she had made when she had agreed to marry him, to tell him if she fell in love with someone else and he would release her from her commitment to himself. But she had already told him that she had nothing to tell him. So what had he meant? To keep the promise she would have to tell him. Not to keep it she would have to. . . . Her thoughts careered to a screeching stop and back-tracked. Not to keep the promise she would have to leave him without telling him she had fallen in love with someone else.

Was that what he had meant? But then she had asked him if he had anything to tell her and he had said 'A lot, but there isn't time.' What had that meant?

Oh, it was all such a muddle, and the more she thought about it the more she became convinced that Rory was trying to tell her that if she left Jura while he was away he would understand that she wanted their marriage to end, and that was what he wanted too.

While she was thinking all this she had cleaned the cottage, and done the washing and dried it so that she could leave the place as soon as she had come to a decision. She was in the bedroom, carefully putting together the pages she had written for him and placing them in a folder, when she heard voices outside the house. The sound of them cheered her. Company for the day would prevent further agonising thought.

'The car's gone,' observed Geordie when she opened the porch door and stepped out into the sunshine to greet the twins. He looked at her, his eyes narrowed in the sunlight. He was playing his favourite role, that of a great detective. 'But you're here—that means Rory can see.'

'You're quite right, Sherlock,' she teased, 'he can.'

'Are you glad or sorry?' demanded Beth in her usual forthright manner.

'Of course I'm glad,' she retorted. Really, these two were far too sharp for their own good.

'You don't look it,' said Beth, 'you look all sad and pale.'

'That's because I've had a cold and I've been cleaning this place,' replied Deirdre.

'A woman's work is never done,' changed Beth, with a grin. 'That's what Mum's always saying. Where's Rory gone, to Craighouse?'

'No, he's gone with friends to Ben Nevis.'

'Oh, bother,' exclaimed Beth. 'Gran sent us over to ask you and him to come to tea this afternoon. You see, Mum and Dad have arrived and Uncle Dougal's in-laws are here. Anyway, you can still come, can't you? I expect you're lonely without Rory. Why didn't you go with him?'

Why indeed! thought Deirdre ruefully, trying to think up an answer to that one. Obviously the twins were conventional in outlook and expected husband and wife to go everywhere together, as possibly their own parents did.

'I stayed behind to pack everything. I might go to London on Saturday,' she explained.

'Oh, then Rory isn't coming back here,' said Geordie, his face clouding with disappointment. 'He'll be going straight to London from Ben Nevis. Mum will be fed up, she was hoping to see him.'

Caught in a trap of her own devising, Deirdre said nothing to correct him. It would be better if the assumption were made that she and Rory would be meeting, possibly in Glasgow on their way south.

'You'll come to tea now, though, won't you?' pleaded Beth. 'And perhaps you'll come with us tomorrow. If it's fine we're going to climb one of the mountains.'

'Yes, I'll come. Will you wait while I get changed?'

As the day was warm Deirdre wore a summer dress of green linen-type material, long waisted, with a pleated skirt. As usual the twins weren't in a hurry, and as they dawdled along the beach all three of them searched for shells. In fact they were so slow that they met Kirsty, neat and pretty in a gay floral dress with a low neckline, coming to look for them.

Immediately she wanted to know where Rory was, and the twins made the explanations while she raised her eyebrows at Deirdre. Then she told them to run ahead and tell Margot that only Deirdre would be coming. They went off in their typical skipping dance, and Kirsty fell into step beside Deirdre.

'Dougal's going to be very interested when he hears you've been deserted,' said Kirsty, and as usual she put emphasis on the word specially chosen to upset Deirdre. Deserted. How well that described how she had felt these last two days.

'What makes you think that?' countered Deirdre rather weakly.

156

'That little scene you and he played out down by the jetty the other day; I'd no idea he could be so demonstrative. Watching him was quite an education,' said Kirsty sarcastically.

'You saw us?' Deirdre was taken aback.

'Yes, Rory and I were coming down the path. He had walked over to the house to find you.' Kirsty stopped and put a hand to her mouth, but above the hand her blue eyes glittered with malice. 'Ach, just be thinking, Deirdre, he probably saw Duncan kiss your hand too. I thought he behaved a little strangely—he suddenly changed his mind and went back up the path. He must hae seen quite a lot one way and another during the past week or so, mustn't he? And you didn't know! Well, well!'

'The past week or so?' exclaimed Deirdre. 'Just what are you getting at, Kirsty?'

'How fierce we are when we're found out, aren't we? Quite the cat, green eyes and all,' mocked Kirsty. 'You know, it occurred to me several times that Rory was not as blind as he made out to be. He's put on a good act and the dark glasses have made it difficult to tell one way or the other, but some things he has done, specially during the last few days, have made me wonder.'

'What things? I didn't notice anything,' muttered Deirdre.

'Perhaps you didn't want to notice,' Kirsty remarked provocatively.

'What do you mean?'

The other girl shrugged her slim shoulders carelessly.

'I'm just guessing, of course. But his blindness made him dependent on you, and while he couldn't see you could hold him, so subconsciously you haven't wanted him to recover his sight. As a result you've tried to ignore any signs of its return, because you knew that once he could see he would leave you—the fact that he's gone would seem to prove that I'm guessing very well these days.'

Deirdre licked dry lips, wishing she could think up some devastating comeback, but all she could say was.

'Because he's gone away for a few days with some friends, doesn't mean to say he has left me for good.'

'No?' Kirsty looked at her pityingly. 'We were all surprised when Rory married you know—he was always self-contained and independent. He didn't need anyone before the accident and blindness didn't change him essentially. It was only something he had to suffer for a while; and who can blame him for taking a summer wife to help alleviate the suffering? But now the suffering is over, he's free again, so he's off to taste that freedom. I doubt very much if he'll come back for *you*.'

The critical blue glance swept over Deirdre as it had done many times before, hinting that Rory could not possibly be attracted by anyone so lacking in obvious beauty.

Kirsty had only put into words what she had spent the last two days suspecting, thought Deirdre miserably as she followed the other woman up the path to the tall, dark house. Because she felt the need for comfort she didn't go with Kirsty to join the group of people sitting about in deck chairs on the small terrace, but went to find Margot in the kitchen.

As usual the kindly woman was there, arranging plates of cold meat for the tea, and being helped by a small wiry woman with cropped black hair and lively brown eyes who could only be the mother of the twins.

'Oh, I'm so glad you've come,' said Margot. 'This is Jean, my daughter. Meet Rory's wife Deirdre, Jean.'

'I've been hearing all about you,' said Jean with a grin, 'and we've just learned that that wild character who is your husband has deserted you for his mistress, the mountain. How long has he been able to see?'

'For a few days, he said. Only he pretended he couldn't, to find out how long it would take us to guess.'

'How like him to tease you all like that, the devious devil,' said Jean. 'I'm sorry to have missed him, though I'm pleased to meet you. We'll have a talk later on, meanwhile come out into the terrace to meet my husband, Murray.'

As soon as she stepped through the french window,

158

Deirdre saw the Carmichaels. They were conversing with Ian Fairlie, and did not notice her arrival.

'What's this I hear about Rory?' asked Dougal, coming up to her after she had been introduced to Murray Whyte.

She told him as they walked over to the stone wall which edged the terrace, and leaned on it to look down at the sturdy two-masted motor-cruiser belonging to the Whytes which swung at its mooring in the shining sun-bright bay.

'So the bridge was nearer than you expected,' Dougal observed slowly. 'How are you going to cross it, Deirdre?'

'I'm leaving the island on Saturday,' she replied. It seemed to her she had arrived at the decision through no effort of her own will it, had been forced on her, all because she had found herself defending Rory's abrupt departure without her to satisfy the curiosity of the twins.

'And you'll meet Rory somewhere?' asked Dougal, cautious as ever.

'Nothing like that has been arranged between us,' she replied.

'I'm also leaving on Saturday,' he said, 'I'll take you to the ferry.'

'Thank you,' she murmured, 'I was going to ask for a lift.'

'I could take you all the way to Glasgow,' he offered. Deirdre hesitated. She didn't want him to get any ideas that she was attainable now that Rory had gone.

'I'll think about it,' she said coolly.

'My, my, you two do look conspiratorial,' mocked Kirsty as she approached them. 'Is some deep plot being hatched?'

'Not that I know of,' replied Dougal. 'Have you met my in-laws yet, Deirdre?'

She shook her head, so he put a hand beneath her elbow and led her past the obviously curious Kirsty and over to the Carmichaels. When Dougal introduced her Bob Carmichael frowned, and fingered his lower lip while his cold blue eyes flicked over her.

'Mallon, Mallon,' he repeated as if having trouble with his memory, while his thin nervous wife nodded vaguely at

159

Deirdre and then glanced away.

'Didn't I see you in the hotel the other night?' The question was rapped out suddenly as the pale eyes steadied on hers.

'Yes. I was with my husband and some friends of his.'

'He was the tall fellow with the reddish-brown hair?'

'Yes.'

'Thought so. You see, I was right, Megan.'

He turned away then to say something to Ian Fairlie and Deirdre felt her cheeks flaming. The snub was obvious, and it had been given because she was Rory's wife. There was no doubt in her mind that Bob Carmichael did not have kindly memories of the young man who had once had the nerve to ask if he could join his climbing expedition.

Bewildered, she turned away to find that Dougal had been drawn aside by Kirsty. But Jean was there, her thin sallow face twisted in a grimace of amazement.

'That was quite something to see,' she whispered taking Deirdre's arm, 'it would seem that Rory is unpopular with some people. Let's sit down and have our chat. You know, I'm finding it difficult to adjust to the idea of Rory as a husband. You're very much in love with him, aren't you?'

The dark eyes were familiar because they were like Dougal's, but they were sharper and shrewder than his, and Deirdre knew she wouldn't be able to hide anything from this tough wiry woman.

'Is it so obvious?' she whispered, a little appalled by the discovery that someone might have noticed something of which she herself had not been aware.

'It is to my mother, who has a way of watching people and drawing conclusions based on her observation, and she usually comes up with the right answer. Don't tell me you didn't know the truth about yourself?'

Deirdre flushed. 'I didn't know I was in love with him until a few days ago, and then I could scarcely believe it.'

'Ach, you're never telling me you didn't marry Rory for love?' exclaimed Jean.

Deirdre shook her head slowly from side to side. Her

eyes were suddenly full of tears and she became engrossed in picking at a thread in the material of her dress with a fingernail.

'Then why?' demanded Jean.

'We married for convenience. He wanted someone to come here and live with him and help him with his book while he couldn't see. Since you know him, you'll be able to guess how desperate he was when he found he was blind—I was afraid he might do something awful if I didn't try to help him, but I couldn't live with him unless . . . you see . . . I have certain principles which I couldn't change.' Deirdre's voice died away, and she still couldn't look up to face those inquisitive dark eyes.

Then she felt a hand patting her knee gently.

'You don't have to say any more, I have those principles too,' smiled Jean comfortingly. 'Lots of us do, and you were right to stick to them. But I'm surprised at Rory.'

'Everyone has been. Perhaps you could tell me why?'

'I'm surprised that he asked you to marry him; it was a big step for him to take. As far as I know he's never committed himself to anyone ever. . . .'

'He hasn't committed himself now,' interrupted Deirdre hastily. 'He isn't in love with me. He doesn't expect the marriage to last, he doesn't expect anything to last. I wish I knew why.'

'I think I know why' said Jean. 'He's afraid.'

'How can you say that? I don't believe he's afraid of anything. He has nerves of steel,' exclaimed Deirdre.

Jean smiled and nodded.

'I know. It seems like that, doesn't it? What I mean is that he's afraid to believe something might last because in his life nothing ever has. He once told me that he never let himself get too fond of anyone, because always when he did that person seemed to be taken from him—so he always kept something of himself back in any relationship, and in that way it wouldn't hurt too much.'

Once again Deirdre became very engrossed in the weave of the material of her dress, because her eyes were swim-

161

ming in tears.

'Thank you for telling me,' she said in a choked voice, 'it explains a lot.'

'I'm glad I've been able to help. Bob Carmichael is still watching you and looking very uncomfortable about something.'

Deirdre pulled herself together. 'Oh. Do you know them well?'

'Not really. He was posted to Singapore soon after Dougal married Sorcha. She was killed fifteen months after the wedding, when Alan was three months old, and they flew back for the funeral. Naturally they were very upset; Sorcha was their only child and had always been something of a problem.'

'I wondered if you knew that Mr Carmichael knew Rory years ago, before he took up photography,' said Deirdre.

'No, I didn't. How did you find out?' Jean looked interested, and Deirdre told her of the incident in the hotel. She added,

'I thought perhaps he met Sorcha at that time.'

'It's a possibility, I suppose, but neither he nor she mentioned having met before.' Jean stopped speaking as a sudden thought struck her. She gave Deirdre a sharp glance and asked, 'Has anyone told you what happened five years ago?'

'Kirsty told me.'

'Poor Kirsty,' Jean sighed. 'How she hated Sorcha!'

'But I thought they were close friends?' exclaimed Deirdre.

'They were, on the surface, it was Kirsty who introduced her unusual, rather fey friend to Dougal. You see, Kirsty and Dougal met when they were both doing post-graduate work at university, and I think she hoped he would ask her to marry him one day. But he fell for those wistful appealing grey eyes of Sorcha's and bang went Kirsty's hopes.'

'I see,' murmured Deirdre. At last she had the key to Kirsty's sourness.

'You may have something in that idea of yours that Rory

and Sorcha had met before—and it could account for their odd behaviour when they met five years ago,' drawled Jean thoughtfully.

'How did they behave?'

'They seemed mesmerised by each other. They couldn't speak. They didn't have to. It was as if they'd known each other in another world. If they met years ago, it explains that feeling we all had about them, doesn't it?'

'Yes, perhaps it does.' Deirdre thought to herself that it didn't explain why Sorcha had followed Rory when he had left the island, but perhaps that was best left hidden.

Meanwhile, she had learned something new about Kirsty. The woman had once hoped to marry Dougal. Watching her at the tea table, being cheerful and occasionally caustically witty, it was hard to tell whether she was still in love with Dougal. But there was no doubt in Deirdre's mind now that Kirsty's experience had made her bitter, and could also have caused her to say what she had said about Sorcha five years ago. She could have been painting her so-called close friend black out of sheer jealousy.

The mention of Rory's name brought her out of her silent musings; Jean had mentioned his mountaineering activities and was asking Bob Carmichael about him.

'You've met him, haven't you?' she said blandly, and across the table she winked at Deirdre.

Bob Carmichael looked a little uncomfortable, gave Deirdre a fierce underbrowed glance and said abruptly,

'Yes, some years ago. He came and asked me if he could go on that expedition I led. I had to turn him down, of course, his experience was negligible. He'd only climbed in this country and there were other things to be taken into consideration too.'

'Sorcha brought him to see us.' Mrs Carmichael's thin throat worked nervously as her husband turned on her, obviously annoyed that she had spoken. 'No, Bob, I'm not going to be quiet about it, although I realise a few feelings may be hurt. She wanted to marry him and you turned him down for that too.'

'Well ... er ... they were too young to know their own minds,' Bob Carmichael defended himself to the silent Fairlies and Deirdre. 'Sorcha was only seventeen and I don't think he was twenty. He had no prospects then; I told him to go away, get some more climbing experience and some money behind him. I told him that when he had both I might consider him seriously as a mountaineer and a son-in-law, and it seems he took my advice. He's not done badly, has he? Got quite a reputation as a photographer, I believe.' He glanced round at everyone as if he expected praise for his treatment of the youthful Rory.

'No, he hasn't done badly,' said Ian Fairlie thoughtfully, 'not when you consider the poor start he had in life.'

'But what about Sorcha?' said Dougal gruffly. 'How did she feel when you sent him away?'

'Well, she grew out of it,' drawled Bob. 'These things don't last when you're seventeen, you know. I expect he grew out of it too.' Here he flicked another rather uncertain glance in Deirdre's direction, as if he were unsure of her reaction.

'I wonder if either of them ever grew out of it,' murmured Jean to Deirdre, as Margot made some conciliatory remark and changed the subject.

Deirdre stayed silent, thinking of Rory. Remembering the shock on his face when she had told him that Sorcha was dead and his refusal to talk about her. She also remembered him saying once he had taken a test and had failed it, and now she knew what that test had been. He had failed to measure up to certain standards which Bob Carmichael held, with regard to mountaineers and prospective sons-in-law.

And later, when Rory had established himself and had acquired the money and experience, he had met Sorcha again too late. By then she had been married to Dougal. So he had gone away again, and had met someone else— Toni—only to lose her too. It was the pattern of his life as described by Jean. Always when he allowed himself to like someone too much, that someone was taken away from him.

But he could have Toni now. Toni was free and waiting for him in London. All he had to do was rid himself of his summer wife and that could be done easily and soon. She, his summer wife, would see to it personally. She would go away before he returned to the island; she would go because she loved him.

The next day being her last on the island, it seemed right to go with Dougal, the twins and Kirsty to climb one of the mountains. Following one of the many burns to its source in a small lake which lay like a fragment of mirror reflecting the sky amongst the dark tussocky moors, they began the ascent up the slippery scree where patches of heather clung and sea-pinks formed spots of delicate colour amongst the barren greys and browns.

They seemed to travel in a haze of golden light which encircled the island like a halo, making it seem an enchanted place chosen for some special happening. Once they disturbed two big birds which took off with a great flapping of wings and noisy squawking. Dougal said they were buzzards, and then pointed to another flight of birds which he said were arctic skuas.

At the top of the mountain there was a stiff breeze which surprised them, because the air had been still and close further down. Deirdre took shelter behind the nest of stones which formed a cairn and rested to recover her breath. She gazed down at the sun-gilded waste of moorland, and seeing the sea, a flat lucid green beneath which rocks and weed showed in purple patches, she experienced a wonderful lift of spirits which was followed immediately by a feeling of regret because she was not sharing this experience with Rory.

Where was he at that moment? Clinging fly-like to some rock face, feeling his way cautiously upward using hands and feet, wholly absorbed in what he was doing, not thinking of her. Oh, having come to this mountain top she could understand now why he loved to climb. It would be to enjoy the sense of achievement, the ecstasy of having pitted wits and strength against something obdurate, and won.

165

'You are saying goodbye to the island, perhaps?' Dougal came to sit beside her. For a second she resented his interruption so fiercely that she felt like pushing him away physically. She did not want him there. She wanted Rory.

'Why do you say that?' she asked.

'You looked sad, as if you don't want to leave. You've been happy here?'

'For a brief time, yes. I have known the richest and the best,' she answered steadily.

'You could know them again, Deirdre, possibly with someone else.'

'I don't want to know them with anyone else.'

'But you will travel with me tomorrow? You'll let me take you to Glasgow?' he urged.

'No, we part at Tarbert. I'll take the ferry to Gourock and travel by train from there to Glasgow, in that way I'll see something of the Firth of Clyde. I might go to Edinburgh, I've always wanted to visit the Castle and Holyrood Palace. I still have some weeks of holiday left, you know.'

He seemed slightly dismayed by this show of independence on her part.

'I don't understand,' he muttered, his dark eyebrows beetling in a frown. 'Deirdre, I was hoping there might be a chance that you and I . . .'

'No.' She was firm and cold, determined to put an end to his hoping; he had no right to hope for anything from her. 'It wouldn't work, Dougal, we're too alike. Why don't you ask Kirsty?'

'Kirsty?' He repeated the name slowly, as if he wondered if he knew anyone of that name, and she felt like giving him a good shake.

'Yes, Kirsty. You know, Sorcha's friend, who loved you and possibly still loves you.' She spoke softly, because Kirsty wasn't very far away, exploring a different part of the summit with the twins.

'You know as well as I do that love has to be returned for it to flourish,' he argued. 'I don't love Kirsty.'

'And you don't love me either. You only see me as someone who would take Alan off your hands, and at the moment you're feeling sorry for me because you think my marriage to Rory is breaking up and I'm miserable about it. Be sorry for Kirsty instead, Dougal, because you and Sorcha between you have made her warped and bitter.'

Deirdre stopped speaking. She was breathing hard, quite surprised at her own forthrightness. Dougal's dark eyes considered her thoughtfully, then glanced away down the mountainside.

'Maybe,' he murmured, and she felt relief flood through her. 'Maybe you're right. You know, I've never given Kirsty much thought.' He rose to his feet. 'It's been a good summer,' he added conversationally, 'and now it's nearly over. We'd best be making our way down now. I'll go and call the others.'

They descended by the north-east slope glissading down the slippery detritus and startling a group of deer which had been grazing, so that the animals all sprang up to stand on rocky outcrops, silhouetted against the sky. As they went lower they could see the U-shaped bay, protected from the sea by the long curving headland. From that height the big dark house looked small and ordinary; beyond it the other bay glinted and smiled, and the white cottage on its shore shone with a mellow, golden glow.

Within two hours Deirdre was turning the key in the door of the cottage, locking it. Reaching up, she placed the key on the ledge so that Rory would find it there when he returned. She didn't allow her mind to linger on that thought, but turned with her cases to put them in the back of Dougal's estate car. Margot had suggested that she should stay the night at Darroch House, in order to make her departure easier in the morning.

Next morning was serene and golden. It seemed to Deirdre as she waited for the ferry to pull out from the pier that the weather was combining with the elusive remote charm of the island to tempt her to stay; to wait for Rory to return and see what happened.

The feeling that she should not be leaving persisted all

the way to the mainland, as the black and white ship with the red and black funnel chugged across the smooth shining water. She stood silent and numb, leaning against the rail on the top deck a little apart from Dougal and Kirsty. She had not been surprised when Kirsty had decided to leave the island too; after all, once Dougal left there was no reason for Kirsty to linger, as she had probably only gone to stay at Darroch House because she knew he would be there.

The green mainland was developing details. Trees, rocks, beaches and cottages took on definite shapes and colours. Soon the ferry entered the sea-loch and slowed down to approach the pier, which was crowded with holi-daymakers bound for the islands.

Once ashore, they had to wait for the car to be hoisted from the ship to the quay. The sun was warm and bright; silvery light danced on the water. Seagulls cackled joyfully and holidaymakers joked and laughed. Everyone and everything seemed to be happy and cheerful, all except herself, thought Deirdre as she stood near the edge of the pier with her hands in the pockets of her suit jacket, and stared down at the shining water.

She felt cut off, alienated from all that was going on around her; she was floating back in time to a day a few weeks ago when her adventure with Rory had begun. Instead of being bright with sunlight the day was dim and damp. Instead of being silver-blue the water was pewter-grey. Instead of being with Kirsty and Dougal she was with a tall man with rust-brown hair who was wearing dark glasses and who spoke in an attractively husky voice.

'Trying your hand at wife-stealing, Dougal?'

Deirdre put a hand to her mouth. Her glance slid sideways in Dougal's direction. Had it happened? Had she gone crazy after all? Had her mind broken down under the strain of the last few days, was she hearing a voice no one else could hear?

CHAPTER-ELEVEN

DOUGAL moved, turning slowly, but it was Kirsty who spoke first, her clear voice shrilling and shrew-like as she went to his defence.

'He isn't stealing your wife,' she said angrily, 'surely three people can travel together without *you* jumping to conclusions?'

'I was only following a trend set by *you* five years ago,' retorted the taunting voice. 'Why should I believe a word you say, Kirsty Brown?' It continued devastatingly, 'You did a good job of smirching my character then, and not a word you said about me was true.'

Deirdre turned then. She wasn't crazy after all. He was really there, tall and rangy, leaning against the bonnet of the seal-grey car, his eyebrows slanting in a frown above eyes which, this morning, held the hard glint of steel.

Kirsty's cheeks were apple-red, and she turned to look appealingly at Dougal, who had transferred his bewildered gaze from Rory to her. Across the space dividing them Deirdre's eyes met Rory's.

'Have you something to tell me *now*?' he asked coldly.

'A lot, but not here with everyone listening,' she said in a low voice, shaken by the sight of him—so unexpected yet so dear and familiar.

'I'm taking this ferry to Port Ellen because there isn't one to Jura today, and I'll cross over the Sound at Port Askaig. If you want to tell me anything it has to be here and now; unless of course you've left a note on the kitchen table.' The final jeer made her flinch.

Dougal and Kirsty had moved away, they seemed to be arguing.

'Rory, I can't explain in a hurry. It's impossible.' Deirdre was conscious of time sliding by inexorably.

'Excuse me, I have to go and see about the car,' he said

169

stiffly.

He turned and loped off with his long hillman's stride to talk to a crewman. Deirdre stood with her heart thumping wildly as the result of having met him unexpectedly, her mind reeling a little under the impact of this new situation. She did not know what to do.

Dougal came over to her carrying her two suitcases, and placed them beside her.

'You won't be coming with us,' he said unemotionally.

'No, I won't. I don't know what I'm going to do.'

'You're going with him. You can't help yourself,' he returned. 'Goodbye, Deirdre.'

'Goodbye, Dougal, and thank you.'

'Nothing to thank me for. We'll meet again another year I expect, on our "dear" island, and who knows, maybe our children will play together and climb the hills together.'

'I hope so. Tell Kirsty . . .' She broke off, then said, 'No, I'll tell her myself.'

Kirsty was already sitting in the seat next to the driver's, and there were traces of dried tears on her face which she was regarding critically in a pocket mirror she had taken from her hand bag. Deirdre leaned down to the open window and spoke quickly.

'Kirsty, I'm sorry Rory was rude to you just now.'

Kirsty looked at her, the blue eyes blurred with tears.

'I deserved it, I suppose. I was jealous of her and then she let Dougal down after he had been so good to her; left him for a man she had only just met, or so I believed at the time.' Kirsty's lips thinned, and her eyes narrowed as she looked into the past. 'You'll know the old saying, Deirdre, about the fury of a scorned woman? Well, I knew that fury twice. Both times because Sorcha came between me and a man. Not content to take Dougal from me she wanted Rory too, so she made sure he never noticed me. I said what I did about them having made an arrangement to meet because I was angry with her for what she had done—not only to Dougal but to me too.' Her voice choked, and she had to clear her throat. 'But it wasn't all lies,' she added, 'Sorcha

170

did follow Rory.'

'But not because he asked her,' Deirdre pointed out. 'That makes the difference, doesn't it? That's the part you left out deliberately.'

'Ach, I admit it. I wanted Rory to suffer too, I wanted to make you suspicious of him. I've tried to make him suspicious of you, too. I've exaggerated your meetings with Dougal, tried to make Rory think they were less innocent than they were.'

'But why, Kirsty? Why?' Deirdre was amazed by this revelation.

'Fury, because five years ago he didn't notice me, yet this year I find him married to a plain, ineffectual overgrown schoolgirl like you.' Kirsty's glance was vindictive. 'And now I can't help but be honest, because you're not coming with Dougal and me. For the first time in years I'll have Dougal to myself.'

'Well, make the most of that time,' retorted Deirdre. She couldn't like Kirsty, but she had to try and help her somehow. It was wrong that anyone so lovely to look at should be so sour within. 'Perhaps I should give you a piece of advice.'

'What's that?' Kirsty looked surprisingly eager to hear it.

'Keep that wasp's tongue of yours under control, and you might get what you want. Goodbye, Kirsty.'

She went back to the place where her cases stood. There was no sign of Rory, and the grey car was being lifted aboard. After a few words with the ticket agent she bought a ticket to Islay, and had her cases carried aboard. Then she climbed up the companionway to the top deck.

The day was fine and clear, and many of the passengers had collected on the upper deck to enjoy the sunshine and views, but eventually she found Rory leaning against the rail. When she leaned beside him he didn't turn or say anything to her. Glancing down at the pier, she saw Dougal raise a hand in farewell before he ducked into the driver's seat of his car; she waved back, he got in and the car moved

171

away.

'Why haven't you gone with them?' Rory's abrupt question revealed that he had been watching.

'I never intended to go all the way with them. I'd decided to take the ferry to Gourock. Remember you suggested that if I wanted to leave before you returned I should ask for a lift to the ferry? Well, that's exactly what happened, Dougal offered me a lift. I thought you said you wouldn't be back until next week.'

'I chanted my mind.'

'Why?'

'Several reasons,' he said laconically.

'You can't have done much climbing.'

'I did enough to discover that I hadn't lost my nerve. I discovered something else too,' he replied curtly.

'Well, I've changed my mind too. I've decided I'd like to go to Islay. I might not get the chance to come this way again, so I might as well see as much as I can' she said lightly.

She knew he turned to look at her, but she kept her glance on the bright water which glinted turquoise and gold under the midday sun.

'Why?' he rapped.

'Oh, several reasons,' she replied airily, in good imitation of the way he had answered her a few minutes ago. Then she gasped as he grasped her shoulders, turning her so that she had to face him.

'Rory, there are other people here and they're watching us,' she warned in a low voice.

'Let 'em watch,' he grated through set teeth, 'they might see more than they bargained for. They might find themselves in the ringside seats at a public wife-beating. Now, tell me! Why have you changed your mind and decided to go to Islay instead of Glasgow?'

Keeping her eyes down, she smiled slightly. She had found suddenly that she could tantalise him as he tantalised her, and that the results were exciting and possibly dangerous.

'I've been told it's a lovely island, soft and green, quite different from Jura—and that there's love and a welcoming there,' she murmured.

His fingers tensed on her shoulders. Looking at him from under her lashes, she noticed that his jaw had hardened, and braced herself for the shaking she was sure he was going to give her.

'Didn't you find love on Jura?' he asked softly.

She shook her head slowly, still not looking directly at him.

'Not the sort I was looking for,' she replied.

He drew in a sharp breath and his hands slid from her shoulders. Looking up, she saw that he had turned to lean on the rail in that familiar pose, head in hands, long fingers clutching at ruffled rust-brown hair as if he were tussling with a problem to which he could not find an answer. She longed to touch his shoulder to ask if she could help, but a sixth sense warned her that such an offer would be rejected out of hand. So instead she said forlornly,

'Of course, if you don't want me I won't come to Islay.' It got through where a more subtle approach would have failed, he raised his head and gave her a narrow searching glance. Now that his eyes were focussing properly he could believe in the idea that the eyes are the mirrors of the soul. Rory's eyes, blue- almost violet-grey, long-lidded and slant-ing upwards slightly at the corners, revealed the proud free spirit which was his.

'I want you,' he said tersely, 'but not against your will. And not if you feel you have to sacrifice yourself for my benefit. You know what I'm like, and now that I'm not blind you have no reason to be sorry for me. You come willingly or not at all, Deirdre.'

He turned away from her and she stood immobile as the engines throbbed and the deck shuddered beneath her feet. Once he had told her he didn't whitewash anything; he wasn't doing that now. In short blunt sentences he had told her how he felt. Now it was up to her.

The power of decision was taken from her as the ferryboat began to reverse away from the pier. Slowly it swung round and pointed seawards.

'Would you like some lunch?' asked Rory. 'I left before breakfast this morning to get here in time for this ferry, so I'm feeling hungry.'

He was so casual about it all, she thought, as she followed him down the companionway and into the dining room. It didn't seem to have occurred to him that the most important decision of her life had just been made for her by the ferry moving away from the pier. There was no going back now.

'What have you been doing while I've been away?' he asked when the food had been ordered, surprising her by opening the conversation first and by showing an interest in her. She responded by telling him about meeting Jean and Murray. Then she remembered the Carmichaels.

'They're still there,' she told him. 'I don't suppose you want to meet them?'

He gave her a wary underbrowed glance, then grinned.

'Can't say I'm keen. I'm not fond of being reminded of past foolishness,' he said.

'So I'd noticed. But it's not unusual to be foolish when you're nineteen, and it's not unusual to fall in love at that age and want to marry the girl,' she replied gently.

'Who told you?' he countered sharply.

'I told Jean about what happened in the hotel, and she asked Mr Carmichael if he knew you. He talked about you asking to go on that expedition, then to the surprise of all of us Mrs Carmichael piped up, and told us about you and Sorcha; how you wanted to get married and how Mr Carmichael wouldn't have you as a son-in-law. That was the test you once talked about, wasn't it?'

'Yes, that was the test,' he admitted curtly, and began to eat.

'Then you must have been surprised when you met Sorcha again and found she was married to Dougal,' she went on. 'Why didn't you tell everyone you'd known her before?'

174

He continued to eat and she had the feeling he wasn't going to answer her question.

'Please will you tell me about it, Rory?' she pleaded. He looked up his eyes empty and cold like a storm-whipped sea.

'I don't see why I should,' he countered. 'It hasn't anything to do with you and me.'

'I can't agree—your relationship with Sorcha has been used by Kirsty to make me suspicious of you, If you'd only explain it a little, I'd feel better. If you'd told somebody you'd known Sorcha previously, there wouldn't have been any misunderstanding of what happened.'

He laid down his knife and fork with a clatter, anger leaping in his eyes.

'Nothing happened. There was nothing to misunderstand,' he retorted. 'Kirsty's imagination was fed by her jealousy of Sorcha. Surely you realise that by now?'

'Yes, possibly, but a person isn't jealous without reason. What was Sorcha like?'

'She was a lovely and unusual person,' he replied cautiously.

'And where did you meet her?'

'In the island of Skye.' He answered laconically, obviously still reluctant to talk about it.

'Had you gone there to climb?' she persisted, seeing that she would have to dig the information out of him.

'Yes. Euan and I had decided to spend our hard-earned two weeks' holiday climbing on the Cuillins.'

'Where did you stay?'

'We camped.' His mouth quirked derisively. 'We couldn't afford hostels or hotels. The Carmichaels were staying at Sligachan, in the hotel—he was teaching Sorcha how to climb.'

'And you met?'

'I met Sorcha only, one day when she was wandering about the moors by herself. She seemed to like me, and when I learnt who her father was I went out of my way to encourage her interest.' He gave her a wary glance. 'I told you once you wouldn't have liked me at all when I was younger. I wanted an introduction to Carmichael and I got it in a way I could never have predicted, knowing my own attitude to marriage. I fell in love with Sorcha, and I wanted her so badly that when she suggested we should get married first, I agreed. It was a wild suggestion, but then both of us were a little wild. On the last day of my holiday, she took me to meet her father.'

He broke off, his face darkening with the memory of what had happened at that meeting, and began to eat with savage concentration.

'I gather his treatment of you was rather brutal,' she said gently.

'He did what he had to do,' he replied coolly. 'He knew Sorcha better than I did. He was wise in the ways of the world, too, and he could see that I wasn't old enough to take that kind of responsibility. He knew that Sorcha needed a husband who could look after her and protect her.'

'Why did she need someone like that?' Deirdre asked.

'Because she was a little unstable mentally,' he replied flatly, and shock ran through her. 'It didn't show much while she was able to have the calm security her parents provided; a security I'd certainly never known in my life, so wouldn't know how to provide. Although I hated Carmichael's guts for what he said to me that afternoon, I've never ceased to be grateful to him. He opened my eyes to reality. From then on I realised that nerve and strength were going to be enough to get me what I wanted in life.'

'But what about your feeling for Sorcha? Did you ever get over it?'

Again he was silent, looking down at his empty plate and fiddling with the handle of the fork, obviously uncertain. He looked up at last with a rueful grin.

'I have to be honest with you, Deirdre. I don't think I did until I met her again. I met other women, but she was always there at the back of my mind, tempting and tantalising, something I'd wanted and hadn't managed to get, I suppose.'

'And what happened when you met her? Were you disappointed to find she was married to Dougal?'

'I was surprised—and then, believe it or not, relieved, to find that he had been able to provide the security she needed. She belonged to him, and suddenly I didn't want her any more.' He paused and rubbed the side of his face thoughtfully. 'If he hadn't gone away without her everything would have been all right, but as soon as the protection he provided was removed she began to visit me. She used to come to the cottage at night and talk about the days we had been together in Skye. I pointed out to her that she shouldn't come, that she was embarrassing me as well as the members of the family who were at the house. She told me she didn't care what they thought, that I was her first love and held a special place in her life. She said she didn't see why we couldn't have a relationship outside her marriage.'

The low husky voice thickened with disgust and Deirdre looked up.

'Didn't that appeal to you?' she asked.

'Not on your life,' he retorted. 'I'm a simple person, I couldn't share another man's wife, nor share my wife with another man.'

This statement of principle on his part both pleased and surprised her at the same time.

'And that's why you left the island,' she said.

'Yes, I removed myself. I'd no idea she would follow me.'

'Perhaps she couldn't help herself,' Deirdre mused sadly. 'Dougal told me that Sorcha always seemed like a child who had been deprived of someone she loved. I think you were that someone, Rory, and when she found you again she couldn't help following.'

'Now you've made me feel more responsible than ever for what happened to her,' he said harshly, rising to his feet and picking up his camera he had set down on the table. 'We must be nearly at Gigha and I want to take some photographs. I'd like you to be in them.'

'Oh!' Her hands went to her hair. 'I'll have to fix my hair.'

'That's up to you.' He gave *her* an appraising, critical glance.

'If you didn't wear it like that you wouldn't have to fix it,' he added cryptically, and strode off without her.

How like him to walk off in the middle of the most important conversation they had ever had, she thought irritably. There was still so much she wanted to know; about Toni; about his reason for returning from Ben Nevis so soon. If he hadn't returned today, what would have happened? Would he have tried to find her in London? Or would he have accepted her departure from Jura as the end to their summer marriage?

It didn't bear thinking about, she decided as she let down her hair in the ladies' room, combed it and tied it back in a ponytail. How youthful the style made her look. Tall, square-shouldered and full-breasted, she didn't look like a suave, well-informed teacher; nor did she look like a house-proud, husband-proud wife. She looked like a dreamy-eyed, overgrown schoolgirl.

Up on the deck she looked for Rory but couldn't find him, so she leaned on the rail and watched people going ashore on to a long pier which jutted out into a wide shallow bay rimmed with golden sand. The scents of flowers and shrubs wafted from the tree-dark island, tempting her to go ashore and explore its peaceful woodlands and empty serene beaches. The water in the bay twinkled with sparks of silvery light and lapped lazily at the hull of the ferryboat.

She stayed there, entranced by the difference the small island offered, and it wasn't until the engines throbbed and the warps were being cast off that she realised Rory had not joined her. Turning, she looked round for him. He was coming down the companionway from the bridge, which was, of course, forbidden to all passengers. Camera slung over one shoulder, he stepped over the rope which was supposed to repel the passengers and came towards her.

178

'I thought you were going to take photographs,' she said.

'I've taken them,' he rejoined.

'Where were you? I couldn't see you.'

'I didn't want you to,' he replied aggravatingly, leaning beside her. 'Time for me to ask a question now. Why were you going to Glasgow today?'

'B . . . B . . . Because I thought you wanted me to leave you,' she stammered. 'I thought you didn't need me any more because you can see. Remember, you only married me for convenience because you needed someone to help you while you were blind.'

'And you only married me because you were sorry for me,' he countered. 'No, don't deny it, I know you did. That's why when my sight came back suddenly, far sooner than I expected, I went on pretending I couldn't see. I didn't want the honeymoon to end before it had properly begun.'

'Then when did your sight come back?' she demanded, turning on him.

'The day you went shopping to Craighouse. It wasn't perfect; I couldn't see small details.' His chuckle of laughter was wicked. 'But you didn't guess. It was when everything became very clear again that I began to wear the dark glasses, in case you did guess. I had to keep you sympathetic towards me somehow, while I taught you how to be a good wife.'

'Oh . . . Oh . . . You cheat, Rory Mallon!' she stuttered, her cheeks glowing with wild-rose pink which he watched as if fascinated. 'I hope you saw a lot you wished you hadn't seen. It would serve you right for playing a trick like that!'

'I did, as a matter of fact,' he said with a wry grin. 'I saw you and Dougal together.'

'But you told me to go walking with him, and when I asked you if you objected you said you valued freedom of action so highly yourself you couldn't deny it to anyone else,' she countered.

'I know I did, and I meant it. Maybe I wouldn't have

thought anything about you and Dougal going off together if it hadn't been for Kirsty's hints; then I saw him kiss your hand. Dougal isn't a demonstrative man as a rule, so I was convinced that there must be something between you. That's why I asked you if you had something to tell me before I left for Ben Nevis. When you said you hadn't, I wondered if perhaps you were afraid to tell me, so I suggested you needn't keep the promise.'

'And I thought you wanted to be rid of me because you'd just learned that Toni hadn't married the American after all. I thought you wanted to go back to her.'

Amazement widened his eyes.

'Go back to Toni? What do you mean?' he demanded.

'She told me once that you and she had an arrangement,' she confessed.

Sunlght was warm on her face. The flat silken sea had a silvery shimmer and beyond the shimmer she could see the softly-rounded slopes of a green island beckoning to her.

'I've never had any sort of arrangement with Toni,' said Rory. 'She's attractive to look at, but there's nothing special about her, at least not for me.'

'Then why did she say that?' said Deirdre, who was by now quite as bewildered as he was.

'I imagine it was to make an impression on you,' he said drily. 'Haven't you ever noticed that Toni has a way of making her relationships with people, or anything that she does, seem more exciting than they really are? It's the way she talks. She did the same when she came to see me that Saturday in hospital. She made out that she had the American on a hook and almost landed, and as we know, it came to nothing in the end.'

'But I thought she'd let you down!' exclaimed Deirdre. 'I thought that was why you asked me to come to Jura with you—because you'd asked her and she'd refused. After all, you did say she wasn't interested in helping a half-blind man.'

'Well, it was true, she wasn't. Not that I would have asked her. You were interested, so I asked you. Ever since

180

Carmichael turned me down on two counts, I've never placed myself in a position where I could be turned down again,' he said with a sardonic twist to his mouth. 'I was going to ask you the last time you came to the hospital, but you wouldn't wait to hear. You rushed off to catch a train and didn't come to see me again. I kept thinking about you, and how useful you'd be, so I had to think up a way of how to get you to come with me.'

His offhand confession of how he had tricked her into coming to Jura with him increased her state of confusion. She gripped the rail hard, holding on to its reality as she watched the green island develop curves and valleys, trees and houses.

'Then why were you upset when I told you what was in Toni's letter?' she asked eventually.

'Was I upset?' he countered. 'I remember thinking you were upset, and thought you were regretting being married to me. What else could I think, when you dashed out of the cottage saying you coudn't stand it any more? I assumed you couldn't stand living with me any more. That's why I reminded you of the promise.'

'You were opening the door for me to leave,' she murmured drearily.

'It was never closed,' he said steadily, 'it isn't closed now. You didn't have to come to Islay today and you don't have to come to Jura with me now. Now that you've found out all you needed to know you can please yourself what you do, Deirdre.'

He turned away as the engines of the ferryboat slowed down. She stood uncertainly, biting her lower lip, and watch him go to the companionway leading to the embarcation deck.

The ferry was sweeping round a green headland turning towards the town of Port Ellen on the shores of a wide bay. Deirdre saw a natural harbour protected from the sea by a breakwater of dark jagged rocks. Harbour buildings glinted white and red in the sunlight which struck sparks from the windows, and the chromium fittings of the buses and cars waiting on the quayside. People were standing about waiting for passengers, occasionally waving or shouting to someone they recognised.

Deirdre forced herself to move at last, towards the companionway. She could see now that she was no different from Sorcha; she had come to Islay because she couldn't help herself. She had followed Rory, but not because he had asked her. And she knew now that he would never ask her again. He had asked her that evening, long ago it seemed, in his studio down by the River Thames. Oh, he had said he wanted her, but he hadn't attempted to persuade her as she would have liked to be persuaded. He hadn't even tried to trick her. He had said she must please herself, go with him willingly or not at all.

Feeling totally without direction, she collected her luggage and staggered ashore with it. Surely if Rory really wanted her to accompany him he would have stayed with her, helped her with the cases? Maybe by now he had gone. While she had stood alone on the top deck she had been aware of the derrick creaking as it unloaded cars and freight.

Seagulls screeched above her head, people chattered and laughed, and with a joyous leap of her heart she saw the seal-grey car a few yards ahead, it's engine growling softly as it waited. Moving almost automatically, she went towards it.

'Put your cases in the back seat,' ordered Rory calmly. He made no effort to help her, and for some reason she did not expect him to. She had to prove to him in some way that she hadn't wanted to leave him, that she didn't regret being married to him.

As the car moved through the small town on the road west, she wished she could have stayed longer to explore. The curves of neat pointed houses, the glimmer of bright sand on the far shore of the harbour, delighted her, but Rory was in a hurry and soon they had left it behind.

Past the white and black buildings of a distillery, past the ruin of a church, past an ancient Celtic stone cross ringed by a wheel of stone carved in high relief. Again Deirdre would have liked to stop and explore, but one glance at Rory's profile, hard and uncommunicative, told her that it was no use even asking. She had chosen to go with him, so she had to put up with the speed at which he drove and his desire to get to Jura.

The road forked beside the well-wooded estate of a country house. Taking the fork to the right, they drove over green rolling country which basked under the warm sun of late August, serene and welcoming inviting the visitor to stay and relax for a while in its pleasant glens.

But Rory wasn't tempted. Soft green curves and lush meadows were not for him; his spirit craved the open moors, the soaring peaks. Silent and preoccupied, he drove on and they came to Port Askaig suddenly, half a dozen white houses gleaming beside the bright waters of the Sound of Islay. Beyond the water lay the 'dear' island, golden-brown moorland rising up to the ample curves of the mountains whose summits appeared suddenly as if in greeting, when the white clouds which had hidden them fell apart and drifted away in fine wisps across the sea.

The small ferry carried them across the narrow swirling waters, and soon they were rounding the tip of the island with the sea on the right twinkling turquoise and gold and the moors purple-shot with heather lifting on the left.

'Did you like Islay?' asked Rory suddenly, the first time he had spoken since they had left Port Ellen.

'You didn't give me any time to find out,' she retorted. 'You came through it like a swift summer storm.'

'I want to get home,' he replied simply.

'Is this where home is?' she asked, feeling excitement begin to stir in her blood. She was beginning a second adventure with him.

He thought about that, his eyebrows slanting in a frown above eyes which seemed more blue than grey in the afternoon light.

'Only if you're there,' he said quietly. 'You've made it home for the past few weeks.'

And the little flame of hope, which had been blown out, was relit. It flickered uncertainly at first, but slowly it steadied and grew brighter, dispersing the shadows of distrust and despair.

Craighouse was quiet and dreaming in the mellow sunlight. Glancing sideways down the road which led to the pier, Deirdre quivered with sudden fear of what might have happened. Only ten hours ago she had stood on the ferry and watched the pier fade from view, thinking she would never see Jura again.

'Supposing we hadn't met in Tarbert today?' she cried out of that terrible fear.

He gave her a brief sidelong glance.

'Stop supposing, love,' he chided softly, 'it doesn't do any good. We met, that's all that matters, and now we're almost home.'

'But if you hadn't returned sooner than you said you would we couldn't have met, and then you'd have thought I'd gone with Dougal. Rory, what made you come back?'

They had reached the place where the lane joined the road and he turned the car on to it before he answered.

'I'm not very good at analysing motives,' he said slowly, 'I want to do something, so I do it. Yesterday afternoon Dick and I were resting on a ledge after we had completed a difficult traverse, and I was feeling pretty pleased with myself because I'd been able to do it without panicking, when I had this very strong feeling—I wanted to be with you.'

'Oh!' she exclaimed. 'I was on top of one of the Bens wishing you were with me.'

'Well, you must have wished very hard, because I couldn't get you out of my mind. For once a woman meant more to me than climbing a mountain did. I had a desperate urge to get back before you could leave Jura.'

'And I was only leaving because I thought you didn't want me any more, when you'd seen how plain and ordinary I am compared with Toni,' she said in a low voice. 'That was the only reason, Rory.'

184

He didn't answer, but the car leapt forward as if he could not bear to linger longer on the way home. Soon the U-shaped bay appeared, shadowed and mysterious even on that sunny day; down they swooped beside it and up again. As they passed the tall dark house, Deirdre saw the twins look up and wave wildly from the garden as they recognised the muted roar of the car.

On the other side of the headland, beside the smiling all-alone bay, the whitewashed cottage glinted. Within seconds the car jerked to a stop in front of it.

Turning towards Rory, Deirdre had a blurred close-up view of his eyes focussing on her mouth, of his mouth clean-cut against the tan of his face. Then everything was blotted out as she felt his lips move against hers. Her eyes closed, her arms went round him, glad to feel the taut muscular bulk of him. Her body seemed to be melting, and she forgot about time.

The mournful mocking cry of a seagull, the soft high of the sea lapping against the shore and the distant babble of the burn were the sounds Deirdre heard as she became aware of time again, the sounds she would always associate with loving Rory.

'Can you believe I don't want you now?' he asked huskily. 'I've wanted you for what you are, not for what you look like, ever since you came to visit me in hospital. I knew what I was doing when I married you. I knew you were a bit above my touch and that you didn't like me, so I had to use your pity to get what I wanted. Then when I could see you I liked what I could see—eyes the colour of shallow sea-pools, skin as white as a cockleshell, hair as dark as a blackbird's feather—and I wanted to keep everything, all the things you are for myself *for ever*. But I'm afraid of that phrase, so I cheated, because I was afraid you'd be taken from me. I was afraid you'd leave me as soon as I could see. Can you forgive me for cheating?'

'There's nothing to forgive,' she whispered, amazed by his jerky confession. 'I can see now that I cheated a little

185

too. And you mustn't say I'm above your touch—I'm part of you now, and you're part of me.'

'Does that mean you can stand staying married to an egotistical ruffian like me?' he asked with a disarming touch of diffidence.

'I know I can't stand living without you. The last few days without you have been awful. I was beginning to think I was going out of my mind. You see, I was sane when I married you. I married you not because I was sorry for you, but because I love you, only I didn't know it at the time.'

'Perhaps that's what's the matter with me,' he said with his sudden taunting grin. 'Would you like me to tell you that I love you, my puritan? Would it make you feel better?'

'It would help enormously,' she said fervently.

'Then let's go in the house. I'm likely to get carried away by my own feelings when I'm telling you, so it would be best if we're behind closed doors. I've a suspicion the twins are on their way here.'

When eventually the twins arrived, the door of the cottage was closed and the only sounds in that tranquil place were the mocking call of a seagull, the soft sigh of the sea and the babble of the burn.

The twins knocked several times and tried the knob of the door. No one answered and the door remained closed. They shouted and whistled and peered in at the windows, but could see nothing through the thick old-fashioned lace curtains. Then after a while they went away, hopping and skipping along the silvery shore, mindful of the warnings their grandmother had given them that it wasn't polite or kind to disturb a newly-married couple like Deirdre and Rory when they were on their honeymoon.

romance is beautiful!

and Harlequin Reader Service
is your passport to the
Heart of Harlequin

Harlequin is the world's leading publisher of romantic fiction novels. If you enjoy the mystery and adventure of romance, then you will want to keep up to date on all of our new monthly releases—eight brand new Romances and four Harlequin Presents.

If you are interested in catching up on exciting and valuable back issues, Harlequin Reader Service offers a wide choice of best-selling novels reissued for your reading enjoyment.

If you want a truly jumbo read and a money-saving value, the Harlequin Omnibus offers three intriguing novels under one cover by one of your favorite authors.

To find out more about Harlequin, the following information will be your passport to the Heart of Harlequin.

collection editions

**Rare Vintage Romance
From Harlequin**

The Harlequin Collection editions have been chosen
from our 400 through 899 series, and comprise some of
our earliest and most sought-after titles. Most of the
novels in this series have not been available since the
original publication and are available now in beautifully
redesigned covers.

When complete, these unique books will comprise the
finest collection of vintage romance novels available.
You will treasure reading and owning this delightful
library of beautiful love stories for many years to come.

For further information, turn to the back of this book and
return the INFORMATION PLEASE coupon.

the omnibus

A Great Idea! Three great romances by the same author, in one deluxe paperback volume.

A Great Value! Almost 600 pages of pure entertainment for only $1.95 per volume.

Essie Summers

Bride in Flight (#933)
...begins on the eve of Kirsty's wedding with the strange phone call that changed her life. Blindly, instinctively Kirsty ran — but even New Zealand wasn't far enough to avoid the complications that followed!

Postscript to Yesterday (#1119)
...Nicola was dirty, exasperated and a little bit frightened. She was in no shape after her amateur mechanics on the car to meet any man, let alone Forbes Westerfield. He was the man who had told her not to come.

Meet on My Ground (#1326)
...is the story of two people in love, separated by pride. Alastair Campbell had money and position — Sarah Macdonald was a girl with pride. But pride was no comfort to her at all after she'd let Alastair go!

Jean S. MacLeod

The Wolf of Heimra (#990)
...Fenella knew that in spite of her love for the island, she had no claim on Heimra yet — until an heir was born. These MacKails were so sure of themselves; they expected everything to come their way.

Summer Island (#1314)
...Cathie's return to Loch Arden was traumatic. She knew she was clinging to the past, refusing to let it go. But change was something you thought of happening in other places — never in your own beloved glen.

Slave of the Wind (#1339)
...Lesley's pleasure on homecoming and meeting the handsome stranger quickly changed to dismay when she discovered that he was Maxwell Croy — the man whose family once owned her home. And Maxwell was determined to get it back again.

Susan Barrie

Marry a Stranger (#1034)
...if she lived to be a hundred, Stacey knew she'd never be more violently in love than she was at this moment. But Edouard had told her bluntly that he would never fall in love with her!

Rose in the Bud (#1168)
...One thing Cathleen learned in Venice: it was highly important to be cautious when a man was a stranger and inhabited a world unfamiliar to her. The more charm he possessed, the more wary she should be!

The Marriage Wheel (#1311)
...Admittedly the job was unusual — lady chauffeur to Humphrey Lestrode; and admittedly Humphrey was high-handed and arrogant. Nevertheless Frederica was enjoying her work at Farthing Hall. Then along came her mother and beautiful sister, Rosaleen, to upset everything.

Violet Winspear

Beloved Tyrant (#1032)
...Monterey was a beautiful place to recuperate. Lyn's job was interesting. Everything, in fact, would have been perfect, Lyn Gilmore thought, if it hadn't been for the hateful Rick Corderas. He made her feel alive again!

Court of the Veils (#1267)
...In the lush plantation on the edge of the Sahara, Roslyn Brant tried very hard to remember her fiancé and her past. But the bitter, disillusioned Duane Hunter refused to believe that she ever was engaged to his cousin, Armand.

Palace of the Peacocks (#1318)
...Suddenly the island, this exotic place that so recently had given her sanctuary, seemed an unlucky place rather than a magical one. She must get away from the cold palace and its ghost — and especially from Ryk van Helden.

Isobel Chace

The Saffron Sky (#1250)
...set in a tiny village skirting the exotic Bangkok, Siam, the small, nervous Myfanwy Jones realizes her most cherished dream, adventure and romance in a far-off land. Two handsome men determine to marry her, but both have the same mysterious reason....

A Handful of Silver (#1306)
...in exciting Rio de Janeiro, city of endless beaches and skyscraper hotels, a battle of wits is waged between Madelaine Delahaye, Pilar Fernandez, the jealous fiancée of her childhood friend, and her handsome, treacherous cousin — Luis da Maestro....

The Damask Rose (#1334)
...Vicki Tremaine flies to the heady atmosphere of Damascus to meet Adam Templeton, fiancé of the rebellious Miriam. But alas, as time passes, Vicki only becomes more attracted to this young Englishman with the steel-like personality....

Jane Arbor

A Girl Named Smith (#1000)
...Mary Smith, a girl with a most uninspired name, a mouselike personality and a decidedly unglamorous appearance. That was how Mary saw herself. If this description had fitted, it would have been a great pleasure to the scheming Leonie Crispin and could have avoided a great deal of misunderstanding between Mary, Leonie and the handsomely attractive Clive Derwent....

Kingfisher Tide (#950)
...Rose Drake was about to realize her most cherished dream — to return to the small village of Maurinaire, France. The idea of managing her aunt's boutique shop produced grand illusions for Rose, but from the very day of her arrival, they were turned to dismay. The man responsible was the town's chief landowner and seigneur, a tyrant — living back in the days of feudalism....

The Cypress Garden (#1336)
...at the Villa Fontana in the Albano Hills in Italy, the young, pretty Alessandra Rhode is subjected to a cruel deception that creates enormous complications in her life. The two handsome brothers who participate pay dearly for their deceit — particularly, the one who falls in love....

Anne Weale

The Sea Waif (#1123)
...it couldn't be, could it? Sara Winchester, the beautiful and talented singer, stood motionless gazing at the painting in the gallery window. As she tried to focus through her tears, her thoughts went racing back to her sixteenth birthday, almost six years ago, and the first time she had set eyes on the sleek black-hulled sloop *Sea Wolf* and its owner, Jonathon "Joe" Logan....

The Feast of Sara (#1007)
...as Joceline read and re-read the almost desperate letter just received from cousin Camilla in France, pleading with Joceline to come and be with her, she sensed that something was terribly wrong. Immediately, she prepared to leave for France, filled with misgivings; afraid of learning the reason for her cousin's frantic plea....

Doctor in Malaya (#914)
...Andrea Fleming desperately wanted to accompany the film crew on the expedition, but Doctor James Ferguson was adamantly opposed, stating that if she went along, he would refuse to guide them. But Guy Ramsey had other ideas, and cunningly devised a scheme whereby Andrea would join them — in a manner the Doctor could do nothing about....

information please

All the Exciting News from
Under the Harlequin Sun

It costs you nothing to receive our news bulletins and intriguing brochures. From our brand new releases to our money-saving 3-in-1 omnibus and valuable best-selling back titles, our information package is sure to be a hit. Don't miss out on any of the exciting details. Send for your Harlequin INFORMATION PLEASE package today.

MAIL COUPON TO

Harlequin Reader Service,
M.P.O. Box 707,
Niagara Falls, New York 14302.

Canadian **SEND** Residents **TO:**

Harlequin Reader Service,
Stratford, Ont. N5A 6W4

Please send me the free Harlequin Information Package

Name _____

Address _____

City _____

State/Prov. _____

Zip/Postal Code _____